HER PLAYBOY
CHALLENGE

HER PLAYBOY CHALLENGE

BY

BARBARA HANNAY

MILLS & BOON®

First published in Great Britain 2003
Large Print edition 2004
Harlequin Mills & Boon Limited,
Eton House, 18-24 Paradise Road,
Richmond, Surrey TW9 1SR

© Barbara Hannay 2003

ISBN 0 263 18073 5

Set in Times Roman 16¾ on 18½ pt.
16-0504-44788

Printed and bound in Great Britain
by Antony Rowe Ltd, Chippenham, Wiltshire

CHAPTER ONE

'MISS SUMMERS.'

From somewhere behind Jen a low-pitched masculine voice called her name. Rich and mellow as dark chocolate, it was a voice that demanded her immediate attention but she had to ignore it. She couldn't let anything distract her.

This was her make or break moment, the first time she was solely in charge of a press conference. Journalists had already started asking their questions. Cameras were rolling.

'Miss Summers, I need to speak to you.' This time there was an edge of impatience in the rumbling baritone.

For heaven's sake! Who in his right mind would interrupt a press conference in full flight? The sound crew guys were scowling, clearly annoyed by the unwelcome intrusion. It was totally inappropriate. Without turning,

Jen raised her hand and made a snappy shooing gesture over her shoulder while she kept her eyes glued on a smirking radio jock, who was shoving a microphone in her client's face.

Her stomach clenched. Her client, Maurice, was famous for throwing tantrums in front of the press. The jock's pugnacious air was exactly the kind of attitude that might set him off. Danger was imminent. Even if the sexy voiced man behind her wanted to tell her she'd won a million dollars he would have to wait.

'Maurice,' the jock crooned, 'you've made a name for yourself styling the hair of celebrities—women who are already beautiful. But today you're opening a chain of suburban salons here in Brisbane. Do you really have something to offer the average woman? When was the last time you *personally* cut an ordinary woman's hair?'

Maurice turned bright pink. 'I have always been a man of the people,' he roared. 'And I'm taking my art to the suburbs!'

The glitter in his narrowed eyes alarmed Jen. Was this a Major Tantrum Alert? She wished she had more experience. This morning her boss had jetted off for a two week holiday in Thailand, leaving only a few vague notes on how to cope. This was Jen's baptism of fire.

To her horror, Maurice suddenly jumped at the jock and grabbed his notebook and, as the cameras whirred, he tore it in half and tossed the ripped pages into the air.

'Here we go!' A reporter near Jen grinned with delight and nudged his neighbour.

'I can cut any woman's hair and make her look like a superstar!' Maurice screeched. 'I can rise to any challenge!'

An excited titter reverberated through the crowd. Jen's heart galloped. It was her job to control this damage, but before she could think of the best approach Maurice turned, lunged forward and grabbed her.

'Look at this!' he shouted, plunging his fingers into her shoulder-length hair. '*This* hair is the definition of ordinary. Ordinary with a capital O.'

Cringe. How mortifying! Every journalist in the salon was grinning at her. She was a PR consultant not a hairdresser's model.

'Don't stop. Keep this running,' a voice from the media pack instructed a cameraman.

Maurice warmed to his attack. 'This woman's hair has no richness of colour. It's mousy and limp.'

Jen groaned inwardly. Unfair. She'd been meaning to have something done with her hair—interesting blonde streaks or a coppery highlight—but over the past month she'd been too busy moving from Sydney to Brisbane and coming to grips with her new job.

'Today's women need hair with good shape and movement. Not this out-of-date style.' Maurice favoured Jen with a grimace that was supposed to be sympathetic. 'Sweetheart, the straight look is *so* last week.'

Was it possible to die of embarrassment? The one time she'd had her hair curled she'd felt like Medusa with a head covered in wriggling snakes. Next minute Maurice would be holding out her split ends to the cameras for close-up shots. But, good grief if she resisted, he could throw a worse tantrum and the conference could erupt into a total shambles. With a sinking stomach, she suspected that she needed to ride this roller coaster to the bitter end.

'Every office girl, every checkout chick has the right to look fabulous and I'm the one to achieve it,' Maurice said as he ran his long slender fingers through her hair. 'Give me challenging raw material like this and I can create a masterpiece in a flash!'

There was a ripple of increasing interest and a few bursts of disbelieving laughter.

Seizing Jen's elbow, Maurice steered her towards a chair in front of a mirror and she squinted as bright lights shone in her eyes and the heat of cameras closed in on her.

Maurice gave a conjurer's flourish as he selected a comb and a pair of scissors. With his other hand he proceeded to ruffle her hair until it fell in a fine curtain over her face.

'*Hold it*. How long is this going to take? I have to speak with Miss Summers. Now!'

Oh, heavens, that dark chocolate voice again.

Jen had completely forgotten the nuisance, but there was his voice. Louder now. And sounding as if he'd lost all patience.

This was beyond embarrassing. How dense was the fellow that he thought he could interrupt such an inflammatory moment?

'Silence!' Maurice shouted. 'I never tolerate intrusion into my art.'

'Well, it's high time you improved your manners, mate,' the voice replied. 'There are some things more important than a haircut.'

Maurice gasped and Jen's head jerked up. With frantic fingers she parted the curtain of her hair so she could gape at the speaker. Heads were turning in his direction, making it easy for her to locate him.

A man in uniform was standing to one side of the salon. A broad-shouldered fellow, big and athletic. She guessed he was in his mid-thirties. He had dark curling hair, dark brows and eyes that were glass-clear, unsmiling and grey. He stood proudly with his feet comfortably apart and his shoulders back.

Like a toreador in a bull ring.

In the pose of a warrior.

And yet…despite the lordly manner there was something incongruous about him. His double-breasted uniform hugged his superb physique like a well-fitted glove, but it was not military issue. Dove grey with dark maroon braid on the shoulders and a company name embroidered on the jacket pocket, it was more the kind of uniform a bell hop might wear.

'How long is this going to take?' he repeated, ignoring the cameras and the open-mouthed journalists. 'I have an urgent delivery for Miss Summers and I can't hang around here all morning.'

Jen frowned. 'A delivery?' He'd disrupted all this for a delivery?

She had no idea who this fellow was or how he had tracked her down. What gave him the right to barge in here?

With a curt motion he stepped aside and made a half-turn towards the salon's main door.

Jen blinked and squinted against the blaze of lights from the cameras. Sweeping away the annoying hair from her eyes, she saw an enormous suitcase and, beside it, a very small girl clutching a miniature violin case.

She blinked again and looked more closely at the little figure and emitted a choked cry. 'Millie?'

Shock sent her jumping to her feet. 'I don't understand.' She swung her gaze from the little girl back to the intruder, then to Maurice's scowling glare and the amused pack of journalists with their pens poised above notepads.

Raising her hands in a gesture of helplessness, she murmured, 'I'm very sorry. If you'd all excuse me for just a moment...' Not looking to right or left, she hurried forward through the crowd. 'What on earth's going on?'

The stranger shrugged. 'I have a little girl here who needs to be given into the care of a family member and I'm told that's you.'

'Who are you?'

'I'm a chauffeur.'

'But you were told to bring my niece here? Who hired you? Oh, heavens, nothing's happened to Lisa, my sister, has it?'

With a glare for the hovering journalists, he stepped closer and lowered his voice. 'She's fine. She rang through to our limousine company from Perth. Seems she's tied up on a job over there and the nanny who looks after the kid has resigned without giving notice.'

The news that Lisa was in Perth didn't surprise Jen. Her glamorous model sister was always dashing off to some distant location. 'The nanny's resigned? Why?'

The man cursed under his breath. 'What difference does it make? Something about a family emergency. My commission was simply to bring the child to you.'

'But this is so inconvenient.'

His lip curled and his expression as he glanced towards Maurice was clearly contemptuous. 'Some people might consider a little girl's welfare more important than what's happening here.' He held out a small notebook with a fancy embossed leather cover. 'This is her schedule.'

'Schedule?'

'Ballet classes, gym classes, music classes, swimming classes.' A cynical, dark eyebrow rose. 'She's probably been signed up for instruction in needlepoint and elocution as well.'

Jen rubbed her forehead. She knew her sister tried to compensate for her frequent absences by keeping her small daughter busy. She glanced once more at Millicent. Oh, goodness, the poor poppet was only five years old and she looked so tiny and lost in this salon filled with strange adults.

Sudden sympathy sent Jen hurrying to crouch beside her little niece. She kissed her and gave her a hug. 'This is a lovely surprise,' she said as warmly as she could.

Millicent didn't reply. She was a plain little thing with light brown stick-straight hair like Jen's and solemn, round eyes that always reminded Jen of the buttons on a rag doll's face.

The child didn't look at all like the famous Lisa Summers, her gorgeous model mother, and Jen had always felt a special soft spot for her. She and Millicent were the very ordinary looking members of the Summers family.

She sighed. It was predictable that Lisa had sent her daughter immediately to her. Everyone always turned to Jen in a crisis. It was what happened to Very Nice People. Her friends and family all relied on her to be a ready shoulder to cry on, a first port in a storm. They'd come to expect her to shove her own needs aside while she willingly helped out…

She'd never minded in the past.

But not now. What a mess. Today of all days. With her boss gone and an entire PR office to run on her own, Jen needed clear space to focus on her own needs, her *own* career.

Her eyes flew back to Maurice and the journalists, who were growing restless. Even rebellious. This had to be the worst possible timing. The momentum of the press conference would collapse like a failed soufflé if she dallied.

As if to prove that point, Maurice's penetrating voice shrilled angrily. 'Jen! We have unfinished business.'

'I'm coming right away,' she called back to him. 'Look,' she said, turning to the limousine driver. 'I'm not sure what to do. As you can see, I'm—I'm very busy.'

His grey eyes rested briefly on her hair and she fancied she saw a flicker of something that might have been amusement. No doubt he agreed with Maurice that her hair was dead awful.

She glared straight back at him. 'I can't possibly deal with this now. You'll have to take Millie to my mother—Caro Summers. She's at 47 Victoria Terrace, St Lucia.'

He shook his head. 'No way. I'm supposed to be—'

'Please!' Jen interrupted, her eyes meeting the challenge of his sharp-eyed scowl. This man was supposed to be a chauffeur, but his manner suggested he was more used to giving orders than taking them. 'You'll *have* to take her there. She's Millicent's grandmother and she's the only solution at the moment.'

She shot an encouraging smile Millicent's way. The poor sweetheart must feel like an unwanted parcel. 'Darling, this man—this—ah—*nice* man—' Turning to the driver again, she asked quickly, 'What did you say your name was?'

'I didn't say.' His jaw hardened. 'It's Harry. Harry Ryder.'

Without warning, the rumbling cadence of his chocolate voice and the penetrating clearness of his grey eyes sent an unwelcome *frisson* skittering through Jen. She switched her attention quickly back to Millicent. 'Harry will drive you to Grandmother's. She'll look after you, and I'll come and get you as soon as I finish work.'

'I haven't agreed to this.'

Inhaling a quick breath, she swung back to Harry. 'But you will, won't you?'

There was an awkward, silent, battling-of-wills moment while they stared each other down. It was broken by Millicent, who walked over to Harry and slipped her small hand into his. He looked down at her, startled.

'Did I hear you say that's Lisa Summers's kid?' yelled a journalist from behind Jen.

She blanched. The last thing she wanted was to divert attention from the opening of Maurice's salons while her famous sister's private affairs were plastered all over the pages of the evening paper.

'Thank you,' she said quickly to Harry, and without looking at him or Millicent again, she hurried back to Maurice and his press conference.

As Harry turned the sleek black limousine on to Coronation Drive he shot a glance into the rear vision mirror and felt a spurt of anger at the sight of the little dot of a child sitting primly on the back seat like a stiff and serious adult. Her grave round eyes were staring past the flashing traffic to the Brisbane River where university students practised rowing.

Her stillness and her quiet acceptance of the morning's strange events disturbed him. Was she used to being passed from pillar to post? She hadn't spoken since he'd first picked her up and he would give anything to know what she was thinking.

Not that it was his role to care. He'd taken this job as a chauffeur because he wanted to observe the lifestyles of the mega-rich and os-tentatious. He wanted to see these types at point-blank range, to get into their heads, in-side their skins. He hadn't expected to like them. And he shouldn't feel sorry for one of their offspring just because she was only five years old and all the adults in her life seemed to have abandoned her.

Three women—all trying to palm her off—the mother, the nanny and now the PR chick in the designer label pinstriped suit—all too preoccupied with their own affairs.

He frowned as he remembered his reaction when Millicent had quietly slipped her hand into his and looked up at him, her strange little button eyes shining with complete trust. He'd felt an unexpected and unwelcome urge to protect her.

He wondered where the men in Millicent's life were.

Jen studied her reflection in the washroom mirror.

Maurice was right. Her hair *was* boring. It was a pity he hadn't followed through with his threat this morning and transformed her into something glamorous and eye-catching. But after the chauffeur's intrusion Maurice had lost interest in her. He'd been too busy being rude to the press.

Not that she wasn't grateful for the way Maurice had single-handedly rescued his own press conference. By randomly insulting and admiring the hairstyles of most of the people present he'd steered interest away from the unwelcome interruption and straight back to himself. The cameras had rolled once more, Maurice had hurled colourful insults left and right and the state of Jen's hair had been forgotten.

Which was fine, except that after her public humiliation she was left feeling self-conscious about her straight, mousy hair. She pulled at a strand and held it up to the light. Yep—split ends, too.

She sighed. Being Lisa Summers's sister meant she'd had a lifetime of living in the shadow of divine beauty. Lisa had it all—height, luxuriant auburn hair, translucent pale skin, almond-shaped deep green eyes and incredible cut-glass cheekbones.

Jen was a plain mouse by comparison—pale brown hair, brown eyes, olive skin and no cheekbones worthy of mention. However, in recent years she thought she'd developed a well-grounded acceptance of who she was and how she looked. Maurice had knocked a fresh dent in her confidence.

Get over it. She turned her back on her reflection, determined to stay upbeat. She was in the midst of turning her life around. She'd moved from Sydney to Brisbane; she'd put her three wasted years with Dominic behind her and she'd left *Girl Talk* magazine to take up this new position with Public Persona.

And now, with so much responsibility suddenly dumped on her, she had to concentrate on preparing brilliant press releases and writing wonderful speeches for her clients. That would be much more important than the condition of her hair.

Nevertheless, she mused as she headed back to her desk, a new image would be the icing on the cake. Looking good was the first step to—

Oh, no! She came to an abrupt halt and her jaw dropped as she shook her head in disbelief.

Harry Ryder stood in the middle of her office, taking up far too much space. He was holding Millicent's hand and he looked mutinous.

CHAPTER TWO

'THERE'S nobody home at your mother's place,' Harry said dryly as Jen hurried towards them.

'Oh.' Her mind raced. Today was Wednesday. Heavens, she should have remembered that her mother played bridge on Wednesdays. She glanced at her watch. It was only two p.m.—hours yet before she could leave work and be free to care for Millicent—otherwise her job would be on the line.

Harry stood with his hands on his hips and nodded towards Millicent. 'The kid didn't seem to have anything for lunch and she was hungry, so I bought her a hot dog. I hope that's OK.'

'Yes,' Jen spluttered. 'Thank you.' She flashed a cautious smile. 'Of course, I'll pay you.' She reached for her handbag.

'Don't bother. The company will put it on the account.' Harry paused and then added, as if he felt compelled to offer some kind of advice, 'Looks like you'll have to ring a child-minding agency. There should be plenty in the phone book.'

'I'm not so sure about that,' Jen said haughtily, conceding that this guy had been helpful, but since when did she take baby-sitting advice from chauffeurs? Especially chauffeurs who didn't look or act like chauffeurs. 'If Lisa wanted to use a child-minding agency she would have organised one herself. My family will take care of her.'

It seemed prudent not to mention that she, her mother and Lisa were the sum total of her family in Brisbane. She held out a hand to Millicent and the little girl came and stood obediently beside her, looking up at her with her strange round eyes that were so innocent and hopeful that Jen felt a distressing lump in her throat.

She squeezed her niece's hand. 'Don't worry, Mills, I'm sure Grandmother will be able to look after you just as soon as she gets home from bridge.'

'I'll be off, then,' Harry said, shrugging. 'Good luck. Bye, Millicent.' He turned towards the door, obviously keen to get away, and suddenly Jen realised she didn't want him to leave. Maybe she didn't want his advice, but how would she cope without him? She had a mountain of work to get through this afternoon.

Harry was almost out the door when Millicent announced loudly, 'I always go to my ballet class on Wednesdays.'

'B—ballet?' Jen repeated faintly.

In the doorway, Harry's hand gripped the lintel, arresting his flight, while the little girl looked from him to Jen and back again with an expectant expression that said very plainly that she trusted these two adults to deal with this new dilemma.

Jen held out a shaking hand to Harry. 'Do you still have Millicent's—um—appointment book?'

'Oh, yeah. Sure. I almost forgot.' His mouth pulled into a wry twist as he extracted the notebook from his hip pocket and handed it to her. 'And her suitcase and violin are just outside in the corridor.'

Jen flicked pages, scanning them rapidly. 'Let me see. Wednesday. Ballet at three p.m. at Miss Zoe's Studio. Second floor, Indooroopilly Shopping Town.'

She bit back a groan and sent a beseeching look Harry's way. 'I don't suppose you could—?'

'Not a chance.' He shook his head and tapped a strong brown finger against the face of his wristwatch. 'I have other clients.'

The phone on Jen's desk rang. 'Please, stay one moment,' she begged as she snatched it up.

'Sydney HQ on line two for you, Jen,' trilled Cleo from the front desk. 'Can you take the call now?'

Oh, heavens. A call from Sydney HQ was like a summons from God. 'Ah—ask them to hold on for just a minute.' Jen dropped the receiver and sent Harry another despairing glance. 'Can I *beg* you to take Millicent to her ballet class? Couldn't you possibly fit her in around your other commitments? I just need help today until I can sort something out. Please!'

Goodness, how many times had she pleaded with this man today?

He stood very still, his wintry, intelligent gaze fixed on her and Jen felt her cheeks grow hot. Surely chauffeurs should look a little more *average*? A weird pulse flickered to life at the base of her throat and she felt an urge to lift the white linen collar of her blouse away from her neck while she fanned herself. She bit her lip and felt thoroughly disconcerted while his critical gaze continued to linger on her.

OK, so he didn't like her, she could live with that, but did he have to make her squirm?

At last he looked Millicent's way once more and Jen was surprised to see signs of warmth creeping into his expression. With obvious reluctance he nodded slowly.

'I'll take her, but after this afternoon she's entirely your responsibility.'

She beamed at him. 'You're a life saver.' Her hand hovered towards the telephone. It was career suicide to keep Sydney HQ waiting, but as her fingers curled around the receiver Millicent's voice piped up.

'Who's going to help me get dressed into my leotard and tights and put my hair up into a bun?'

Oh, crumbs! Jen couldn't hold back a groan of utter frustration. Eyes closed, she sagged against the desk, her head full of dark thoughts about the nanny who'd chosen today of all days to pull the plug. Then she heard Harry's chuckle and her eyes flew open again.

'This is one task I'm absolutely certain I can't help you with,' he said. He was grinning and the skin around his eyes creased with genuine merriment as if he were enjoying her predicament.

Jen felt a hot rush of anger which lasted all of three seconds before her own sense of humour kicked in. Hey, she was usually the one who saw the funny side of things. And now she saw the element of the absurd in the way today's events kept snowballing. She couldn't help smiling back.

She was still smiling at Harry as she lifted the phone and spoke to Cleo. 'I'm sorry, but I'll have to call back later,' she said. 'I have an emergency here.'

Harry Ryder wondered about Jen Summers's smile as he drove Millicent to her ballet class. Perhaps she wasn't quite the self-absorbed corporate wunderkind he'd first thought. This morning he'd had her pegged as unsympathetic to children, the kind of new-age, power-tripping woman who'd worn a double-breasted, pinstriped suit to kindergarten and had grown up to view children as lifestyle-threatening parasites to be avoided at any cost.

But when he'd returned to her office she'd seemed to genuinely care about Millicent and the way she got the kid kitted out for her ballet class was nothing short of miraculous as far as he was concerned.

And then there'd been the way she'd smiled. Smiled and laughed. Her brown eyes had lit up and her face had changed completely. And, if that hadn't intrigued Harry, he'd looked clear into her eyes and seen that they didn't quite match. She had a piece of gold, a fascinating pie-shaped triangle, in her left eye, like a slice of ginger amidst the nutmeg-brown.

And somehow that delightful imperfection made her smile unforgettable. To his complete bewilderment, Jen Summers lingered in his mind. It didn't make sense because, as that hairdresser had so loudly pointed out, she was plain—not Harry's kind of woman at all.

Jen's afternoon went from whirlwind to cyclone.

Not that she wasn't used to being busy. In the month she'd been in this job she'd discovered that her boss, Tamara, liked to indulge in long lunches and to hobnob at every available cocktail party while Jen stayed back in the office and slogged.

But Tamara's strength was that she was good at handling Sydney HQ. She didn't let them bully her.

Jen wasn't quite so thick-skinned and, after an afternoon of heavy demands from Sydney, she felt bludgeoned to a pulp. To make matters worse, Harry Ryder was late getting back with Millicent.

By the time she glanced at the clock it was after five already. The ballet class would have finished an hour ago and, despite peak hour traffic, they should have been back by now. She crossed to the window of her third floor office and peered down into the busy street below.

The traffic was crawling at a snail's pace, so perhaps Harry had been held up in a jam. She shouldn't panic yet.

After all, Harry Ryder was from a reputable limousine company. He would be an expert driver and Millicent was perfectly safe in his care.

Nevertheless alarm prickled in her stomach and, as she turned back to her desk, she chewed her lower lip. There was something different about Harry....

A person in a blindfold could sense the difference. Even without his princely posture and his proud manner, his rich, commanding voice suggested centre stage.

He was an enigma that bothered Jen. Especially now...She wouldn't be happy until Millicent returned.

Where were they?

She glanced outside again. It was growing dark and, as she paced her office, she could see lights coming on all over the city.

Her head whirled with questions. Had there been an accident? Had Harry understood that he couldn't just drop Millicent off in the shopping centre's huge car park and leave her to find her own way to ballet? Was the little girl lost?

Perhaps Harry had gone off to do another job and forgotten about the child. *Could she trust him?*

She stopped pacing as a wave of panic engulfed her. Heavens, she'd entrusted her niece to a man she knew nothing about. And, on the two occasions she'd been with him, she'd felt there was something very different about him—an element of danger. She eyed the phone sitting on her desk. Should she telephone his company?

Horrible images flashed in her head—a car smash—she was sure she'd read somewhere that dusk was the most common time of day for road accidents. She could picture Millicent in an ambulance, her leotard soaked with blood. She could see the poor little girl lost in Indooroopilly Shopping Town, terrified and crying. Millicent left alone and abandoned somewhere in the back of Harry's limo.

Her sister had trusted her daughter into her care and Jen knew she would never forgive herself if anything happened to the child.

She'd never felt so sick with fear. *What has happened?* Now, even the thought of ringing the limousine company that employed Harry Ryder filled her with dread. Harry *who*? she imagined them asking.

What was wrong with her? Normally she was a cool, in control kind of person. She began to shake. *I'm having a panic attack!*

'I have to go,' said Millicent.

'Go where?' Harry asked, frustration mounting. It had been bad enough when he'd been delayed on a job by a client who'd taken much longer than expected. Then he'd been caught up in traffic, and when he'd arrived late to pick up Millicent from ballet Miss Zoe's disapproving stare had let him know that his lack of punctuality was unforgivable.

Now he was trying to hurry the child through the crowded shopping centre and back to the car park, fully aware that he would have to face Jen's anger as well. How the blazes did he let himself get tied up in this?

'I need to go to the toilet.'

Hell.

Still dressed in her tiny blue leotard and pink tights, Millicent was holding his hand as they took an escalator to the ground floor but her face was turning pink with concentration as she stood with her legs crossed, knees pressed tightly together.

'Doesn't Miss Zoe have toilets at ballet? Why didn't you go there? You had plenty of time.'

'I didn't *need* to go then.' Her little face screwed up into a picture of agony. 'But I have to now!'

'OK, OK.' Harry felt his brow bead with sweat. This was a crisis way out of his field of experience. He certainly hadn't expected anything of this nature when he signed up for a month as a chauffeur. 'Hang on. I'll find you a toilet.'

When the escalator reached the ground floor he decided that the less walking Millicent had to do the better and he lifted her into his arms. Scanning the ground floor mall, he quickly found the appropriate signs, headed for the door of the Ladies Room and then, relieved that they'd made it safely, set her down.

Millicent looked up at him. 'Aren't you going to come in with me?'

'Er... No, sorry, kitten, I can't.'

She looked as if she didn't believe him.

'They don't let men in the ladies' rooms,' he explained, summoning a reserve of patience he hadn't known he had. 'You'll be OK. I'll wait right here by the door. You—er—you know what to do, don't you?'

Millicent nodded, but she didn't look as confident as Harry would have liked and she seemed incredibly tiny as she disappeared inside.

Harry waited by the door like a bouncer on guard outside a nightclub and a middle-aged woman standing nearby gave him a very suspicious glare. He resisted the temptation to glare back at her and sent her a winning smile instead.

Suddenly Millicent was back in the doorway, tugging at the leg of his trousers.

'Good girl.' He beamed at her. 'That was quick.'

'I haven't *been* yet. I need you to help me take my leotard off.'

Harry gulped. 'Really?'

She nodded. 'And hurry, *please*.'

Sweat broke out. He glanced at the woman waiting nearby. 'Excuse me,' he called in his most charming manner. 'Could you possibly help us?'

The charm must have worked. When he explained his dilemma she seemed only too delighted to help.

'Young fathers are wonderful these days, but there are some things they still can't manage, aren't there?'

She was quite pink with pleasure as she hurried inside with Millicent. When they re-emerged the little girl's face shone with triumph and Harry couldn't remember the last time he'd felt so relieved.

Mission accomplished.

There was a sound outside and Jen jumped, then she heard a girlish giggle and she hurled herself through the office doorway and into the corridor.

Harry and Millicent were walking towards her hand in hand. *Oh, thank heavens.*

She hurried forward and almost pounced on Millicent, hugging her fiercely. 'Are you all right, darling?'

The child nodded and Jen knelt beside her and studied her face carefully, searching for signs of fear or distress, but Millicent looked quite happy.

'What on earth happened?' Jen asked them. 'I've been out of my mind with worry.'

'The traffic—' Harry began.

'I needed to *go*,' said Millicent.

Jen felt her body grow limp with relief. *Don't ever let me become a parent. I couldn't bear to go through this terror every time a child was late home.*

She hugged Millicent again and then moved to hug Harry. 'Thank you,' she cried and she almost flung her arms around him.

But he frowned and seemed to spring to attention, becoming super still. Just in time, she stepped back, dropping her arms to her sides, suddenly hot and flustered and way too conscious again of Harry as a man. A helpful and incredibly *masculine* man. The mega-manly kind of guy who made girls go weak at the knees—a complete pheromone factory, in fact.

What had she been thinking? A package like that wouldn't welcome plain Jen Summers throwing her arms around him.

'Sorry we're late,' Harry said abruptly. 'I hadn't picked you as someone who'd panic.' He dipped his head so that his grey eyes were close to hers and something deep and searching in his expression sent her silly heartbeats scampering. 'Are you OK? You look white.'

'I'm fine,' Jen murmured, pressing one hand to her chest and another to her quivering stomach. 'You're right. I panicked. Silly, I know.' She leant against the wall and took a deep breath. 'And I've been so busy today I skipped lunch, so I guess I'm feeling a little light-headed.'

She straightened again. 'But thank you for helping me out today, Harry. I know it was above and beyond the call of duty.' She drew another deeper breath. 'I guess you'll be wanting to head off now.'

He nodded.

She looked down at Millicent. 'And we'll go out to Grandmother's.'

'How will you get there?' Harry asked.

'I have my car.'

'You look shaky on your pins,' he said, frowning. 'Why don't you let me drive you? St Lucia isn't far out of my way.'

She stared at him, completely surprised by his offer. He looked a bit stunned himself, as if he already regretted his generosity. She felt fine really and it was on the tip of her tongue to decline, but then she remembered that she hadn't consulted her mother about the week ahead yet and, given her own hectic schedule, Harry Ryder and his limousine were still valuable commodities she should keep on hand for as long as possible.

'You don't have any other trips to make this evening?'

He shook his head. 'I'm finished for today.'

'Well, then, thank you, Harry. Let's get Millicent's things.'

*   *   *

'Darling, I'd love to help out. You know I'd give anything to have dear little Millicent stay here, but I'm so sorry, I'm fully booked up this week. Such a *shame*.'

Caro Summers sat on her rose-pink, silk brocade sofa with Millicent on her lap and a woefully apologetic look on her attractive face.

And Jen smelled a rat.

Her mother was playing games. Matchmaking in all probability. When Caro had opened her front door to find her younger daughter with Harry and Millicent on her doorstep, her eyes had widened with momentary shock followed swiftly by pure pleasure.

She'd been quite brazen in her visual appraisal and approval of Harry. The chauffeur's uniform hadn't put her off at all. Not for one beat.

Now she kept taking surreptitious peeks at him as he lounged, ominously silent and brooding, in an opposite chair.

Jen sighed. It was bad enough that her mother and Lisa had hogged all the beauty genes in the family, but it was a zillion times worse when Caro took pity on Jen and tried to help.

Simply because Jen had been going through a date drought since she'd moved back to Brisbane after breaking up with Dominic, her mother saw it as her responsibility to pair her off with every available male. Jen knew that a matchmaking scheme was ticking over in Caro's head now.

'You must have taken on a lot of extra charity work if you're tied up *all* week, Mother,' Jen suggested darkly.

'Oh, I have, darling. So many people depend on me,' she said, all innocence. Caro gave Millicent a squeeze. 'And you'd have so much more fun with Auntie Jen and Harry, wouldn't you, poppet?'

Millicent gave a tiny, cautious nod.

'But I have a full-time job!' Jen exclaimed.

Caro smiled sweetly. 'Perhaps Harry…?'

'Harry is fully committed, too.'

Jen jumped to her feet. Millicent was yawning and her mother was going too far this time. Harry was virtually a stranger. She crossed the room and took Millicent's hand. The poor child looked exhausted and she had to be feeling very insecure, hearing her future discussed like this. She needed her tea and a warm bath and to be tucked into bed. 'It's a shame you're tied up, but thanks anyhow, Mum. I'll work something out. Come on, Mills. Let's go home and I'll cook something yummy for your dinner.'

Caro beamed at her. 'I'm sure you and Harry will sort everything out between you.' She rose majestically and shone an incandescent smile Harry's way. 'Won't you, Harry?'

He mumbled something incomprehensible.

Outside, Jen said to Harry, 'Can I sit in the front? I need to discuss a few things.'

Again his response was inaudible, but she clambered into the front seat anyhow. It was strange enough being driven around in this enormous limousine without being stuck way in the back. Once they were on the road Harry was quite articulate.

'What is it with your family? I've never met so many busy women.' His usually sonorous voice was sharp with derision. 'First your sister and her nanny, then you, now your mother—'

He stopped abruptly in mid-sentence and Jen sensed he'd bitten off the rest of his tirade before he said something really rude.

She didn't bother to answer. It was hard to rise to her family's defence when she was still so angry with her mother.

Harry cocked his head towards the back seat where Millicent sat reading her book and, lowering his voice, he sounded genuinely concerned when he asked, 'No father in the picture?'

Jen shook her head and said quietly, 'Lisa's been very hush-hush about him. I honestly don't know the full story there.'

She had her suspicions. Six years ago, Lisa had been madly in love with a musician, a concert pianist, but as far as Jen could tell they'd both been so busy with their careers that they'd never 'got it together'. Jen had often wondered if the man even knew about Millicent.

But she wasn't about to share that with a chauffeur she'd only just met. Hurrying to change the subject, she added, 'We need to sort out how we're going to handle this babysitting dilemma.'

'*We* need to sort it out?' Harry sent her a scoffing look. 'Listen, Miss Summers, this is your dilemma, not *ours*.'

Her chin tilted stubbornly. 'But you'll help, won't you? If I pay you extra?'

''Fraid not.'

No way.

Harry stared straight ahead, avoiding the pleading in her eyes. He'd already made enough soft decisions today. Time to call a halt. When he'd taken this job his aim had been research. He wanted to meet and observe high-flyers, the mega-rich divas who chose to be transported in chauffeur-driven limos. He'd even hoped there might be one or two criminal types among his clients. So far it had been rather disappointing and no way did he want to get bogged down in a tame stint like babysitting.

'Sorry,' he said. 'As I told you earlier, you need to ring an agency.'

Jen saw no point in replying. It was completely dark now and she sat in an exhausted daze as the lights of traffic and neon signs flashed starkly against the black night and they travelled in silence back to the inner city. She directed Harry to the multi-storey car park where she'd left her car and when they reached it he transferred Millicent's suitcase and violin from his limousine to her Volkswagen.

'You've been a very, very good girl,' she told the patient Millicent as she settled her on to the back seat of her car and secured the seat-belt. 'Are you hungry?'

Millicent nodded.

'Do you like spaghetti and meatballs?'

'Yes.'

'Terrific.' Jen dropped a kiss on her forehead, grateful that she could get away with cooking something very simple this evening.

As she straightened again Millicent said, 'I haven't practised today.'

'Practised?'

'My violin.'

Oh, heavens. Jen stared at her in semi-horror. A five-year-old did violin practice and worried if she missed *one* day? What had happened to innocent, carefree childhood? 'Maybe you can skip practice this once.'

Millicent looked anxious.

'Well—' Jen sighed '—if you're not too tired, I guess you can do a little practice when we get home.'

As she walked round to the driver's door she pressed shaky fingers to her throbbing temples. She felt awful—tired and hungry from skipping lunch and she had a headache. And now there would be the joys of a pre-schooler scraping away at a violin as well. *Can I stand it?*

How was she going to handle the responsibility of Millicent *and* her huge workload? And not a word from Lisa. Typical! She felt at her wits' end.

Turning, she lifted a hand, planning to wave goodbye to Harry, but he was too busy talking into a mobile phone to notice. A sigh of frustration escaped her. How crazy of her to have hoped that she could persuade him to help.

The day's events and the weight of the hectic fortnight ahead pressed down on her like a heavy suffocating fog and she stood with her hand on the driver's door handle, willing herself to find the strength to get into the car, to drive home, cook dinner…

There were footsteps behind her and she turned wearily to see Harry approaching.

'I just rang our office to see if there was anyone else who could help you out,' he said.

'Oh, thanks.' She summoned a weak but grateful smile. 'Did you have any luck?'

'No go, I'm afraid. All the permanent staff have regular commitments and they couldn't accommodate Millicent's broken-up schedule.'

'Well, thanks for trying anyway.' She frowned as she looked at him. 'So you're not part of their permanent staff?'

'No.' Without further explanation, he stepped back and raised his hand in a half-hearted gesture of farewell. But then he raked that same hand through his rough, dark curls and grimaced as if there was something else he needed to say but the words were difficult to get out.

His discomfort intrigued her.

'Damn it,' he said suddenly, as if giving in to the struggle. 'I'll do it. I'm your man.'

'My man?' Jen echoed faintly, not daring to hope.

His mouth tilted into a crooked half-smile. 'I'll be Millicent's driver.'

'Oh, Harry!' Tears threatened. Crazy, embarrassing tears. 'You wonderful, wonderful man!' The flood of relief sweeping through her was so strong she threw her arms around him, hugging him tight. 'How can I thank you?' He was big and strong and smelled sexy and—

Harry's hands touched her waist very tentatively and he made an uncomfortable, throat-clearing sound.

'Oh, goodness.' Jen pulled back, her face aflame. Why did she keep wanting to throw her arms around this man? 'Sorry—I got carried away for a moment. I'm just so relieved to have your help. I've got so much happening at work at the moment and I—'

'It's OK,' Harry cut in, holding his hands away and reversing towards his car. He ducked his head and waved to Millicent in the back of Jen's car. 'See you tomorrow, Duchess.'

'See you, Harry,' Millicent called back, smiling broadly.

Jen dragged in a deep breath and made a business of fiddling with her door handle but she didn't call goodbye. She'd already said more than enough.

CHAPTER THREE

JEN hit the office next morning to find that Sandi from Sydney HQ had already called twice.

'Listen, Jen, we need you to manage a book launch for a hotshot thriller writer. We usually handle his promotions from Sydney or Melbourne and we didn't realise till today that he's in Brisbane at the moment, so it's all going to happen from there.'

And good morning to you, too, Sandi. 'When?' Jen asked, reaching for her diary.

'Monday afternoon, two p.m. at Lawson's Bookstore.'

'Monday? Gosh, Sandi, I'm up to my ears preparing statements for the chairman of Fortune Bank. Their AGM is Monday morning and, with all the wild speculation in the press about them being on the verge of collapse, I've got my work cut out.'

'You can handle both, Jen. There won't be a lot of prep required for this book launch. The author's already written half a dozen books and is used to handling the media. I'll send through some background details and you just need to put together a basic press release and organise some simple catering. You can knock it over in no time.'

'Who is this author?'

'H R Taggart.'

'Mmm…I think I've heard of him, but I haven't read anything of his. I presume H R is a guy, or is he female?'

There was a muffled snort on the other end. 'Taggart's a guy. Writes bloodthirsty thrillers. A blokey kind of writer, and a bestseller, so he needs special treatment. His publishers are Eagle and Browne and their account is important to us.'

'OK.'

'This new book you'll be launching is called *Dead Certainty*. Eagle and Browne have sent all the books, posters, bookmarks et cetera directly to Lawson's and I'll e-mail you what background we have on him. OK?'

'Sure,' Jen said, forcing herself to sound confident in spite of a thousand misgivings. 'I'll give it my best shot.'

She hung up and slumped in her chair, wondering if she could cope with the jobs that were piling up. She was already dreading Monday morning. She'd heard on the grapevine that Gerald Harvison, chairman of Fortune Banking Corporation, was somewhat lacking in the charisma department. Apparently, he was easily upset by bolshie questions from journalists, so she had a lot of work ahead of her, going through the media monitoring files and preparing the most aggressive questions he might have to face, so that she could brief him before the meeting.

Heavens, she was only just coping with the work her boss had left and now this extra job could sink her. And she now had Millicent to look after as well.

Right now, Millicent was in the little room off Jen's office playing computer games until it was time for her music lesson. At least she was a good kid. For that Jen was extremely grateful. And another lucky break had come when Jen phoned the music teacher and the dear woman volunteered to keep Millicent at her place for the rest of the day so that she could play with her daughter.

But, on top of work and Millicent, there was Harry Ryder, who shouldn't be an issue but somehow was. Jen flinched at the memory of the way she'd thrown herself at him last night and then made it worse by leaping away afterwards, blushing furiously, stammering and flapping like a twitty schoolgirl.

No doubt she'd overreacted because she hadn't been in another man's arms since she broke up with Dominic. Problem was—from memory, hugging Dominic had never been anywhere near so…unnerving. So electrifying. Not even when they had first met.

The memory of hugging Harry had bothered her all evening and it had kept her awake last night. It was so maddening. She'd been exhausted and yet she'd lain wide awake, thinking about Harry.

He was a menace to a girl's inner peace but, unfortunately, she needed him.

'Harry, my dear boy, who's this young lady you've brought to visit?'

Harry bent to kiss his grandmother's silky cheek. 'This is Millicent. Millicent, I'd like you to meet my Gran, Polly McLean.'

'Hello,' Millicent said and her button eyes widened as her smooth, plump five-year-old hand was clasped by thin and wrinkled eighty-three-year-old fingers.

'I'm driving Millicent to her violin lesson and, as we were passing, I thought I'd drop in quickly to make sure you're behaving your-self.'

Polly winked at Millicent. 'Is my grandson a good driver?'

'Yes,' said the child gravely. 'He's already taken me to ballet and my grandma's and to Jen's work and we didn't crash once.'

'Well, that's a relief,' Polly said with a laugh. Then her head tipped to one side and her brown eyes sparkled as she said, 'Ballet, your grandmother's house, Jen and now violin practice. You're a very busy young lady, aren't you?'

Millicent shrugged.

'What about this Jen you mentioned? Is she a little friend of yours?'

'She's not little, she's a lady. She's my auntie.'

'Oh, I see,' Polly said in a voice rippling with a marked curiosity that made Harry suddenly nervous.

Millicent sent him a dimpling smile and then whispered to Polly, 'I think Jen might be Harry's girlfriend.'

'Oh,' said Polly again and her eyes brightened as she glanced up at her grandson.

'Don't even think it,' Harry said hastily. *Where the hell has the kid got that idea from?* 'Jen is helping her sister out with baby-sitting. The nanny resigned. It's a long story. You don't really want to know, but I'm simply helping with the driving.'

Polly regarded him thoughtfully, then sighed. 'My boy, I take comfort in the fact that you're a perfect gentleman with old ladies and now, it seems, with little young ladies too. However, it's the age group in between that perpetually worries me. Don't you do anything to upset Millicent's Jen.'

Harry's lip curled. 'Believe me, Grandmother, Millicent's Jen is perfectly safe.'

'Mmm,' mused Polly. She pointed to a newspaper on the coffee table. 'I've just been reading that the experts are now saying that remaining single is as bad for a man's health as smoking. Almost every test shows that bachelors don't live as long as married men.'

'That's fascinating,' Harry mumbled and he glanced at his watch.

Millicent had wandered over to study a glass-fronted display case of porcelain figurines. Polly turned her sharp gaze Harry's way. 'Does Millicent's Jen know who you really are?'

Harry sighed. Polly was in one of *those* moods. 'Jen knows I'm a chauffeur. It's what I am and what I will be for another week. She doesn't need to know more. Anything else will only complicate matters.'

'I hope it won't complicate how she feels about you,' Polly said, leaning towards him.

'For heaven's sake don't start that now. And don't listen to a five-year-old. I've told you there's nothing—*absolutely nothing*—happening between us.'

'Mmm,' she said again. 'Intelligent children can be astonishingly perceptive.'

'And they can be fanciful,' said Harry.

Polly sat very still with her mouth tight as if drawn in by purse strings, her gaze following Millicent as she wandered to the far end of the room to look at the collection of ceramic birds. 'You know I don't like subterfuge. It worries me. Honesty is always the best policy.'

'Trust me on this one,' Harry said, hanging on to his patience by a thread. 'In a few more days Millicent's mother will come back to Brisbane and hire a new nanny. Millicent will go home, Jen will get her life back and, shortly after that, I'll stop chauffeuring. None of us will see each other again, so Jen doesn't need to know anything else about me.'

Polly didn't look at all convinced. 'I'm not sure you should rely on things staying that simple, Harry.'

'Why are we having this conversation? What do you know about any of this? You haven't even met Jen.'

'No,' she conceded, 'that's very true.' She looked up at him with a wistful smile. 'But I know you very well, dear boy, and that's what worries me.'

That evening the summer-sweet smell of frangipani lingered on the hot, still air as Harry stood before Jen's front door and tried to ignore his uneasy tension.

Her house wasn't anything like he'd expected. Somehow he'd figured a super-slick career chick like Jen would rent a trendy inner city yuppie apartment, but this rambling old timber Queenslander clinging to the side of Red Hill was a home from his grandmother's era and it had the cared-for, lived-in-and-loved ambience of Polly's house too.

Coming here was a mistake. Harry didn't mess with domesticity. If Millicent hadn't left her violin in his car, he would have avoided Jen's house like the plague.

It was all so very cosy.

Harry Ryder didn't do cosy.

Why couldn't she have preferred concrete and glass and chrome? *I can't believe I'm letting this get to me. She's nobody—just a client.*

A fat ginger tabby cat strolled down the verandah and greeted him with a lazy, yawning meow.

'G'day, mate,' Harry murmured, almost under his breath. He moved towards the door and the cat stayed close, trying to rub his head against Harry's ankles in the manner of all cats at teatime. From inside came the sound of classical music...something elegant and emotive. Elgar. And Harry could smell dinner cooking—a wholesome, old-fashioned smell he couldn't quite pin down.

He fancied he could hear laughter—two bell-like tones—Millicent's tinkling giggle and Jen's warmer chuckle. A woman and a little girl. *Jeez. Happy Families.*

Golden and ruby light glowed from behind the circular stained-glass panel in the front door. On either side of the door stretched deep, immaculately swept verandahs enclosed by white lattice. A wrought-iron table near the door held a lighted citronella candle, old gardening gloves, a trowel and an empty terracotta pot. At the far end of the verandah a canary sang in a cage amidst enormous tubs of maidenhair fern and hanging baskets overflowing with pink begonias.

He was nervous, gripped by an uncharacteristic caution—not his usual behaviour when visiting a young woman—so nervous he dragged in a deep breath and turned to leave. *I could prop the violin by the door, press the doorbell and do a runner.*

Who would have thought? Harry Ryder, the guy who'd always lived on the wild side, running from a woman, a little girl and a house…

He glanced back out to the street…and safety. Night was closing in on the suburbs. Two doors away a woman called her children home from their play. A middle-aged man with a briefcase and a newspaper under his arm whistled lightly as he walked down the hill from the bus stop. Across the street a television flickered through a front window. In the distance lightning flashed above Mount Coot-tha. A summer storm was brewing.

Best to get this over with.

Shoulders back, he stepped towards the door and raised his fist to knock, but it opened while his hand was in mid-air.

'Harry!'

Jen looked shocked to see him and she gripped the doorknob tightly as she stared at him. 'I was coming to let Sidney in for his tea.' The cat pushed past her legs and disappeared inside the house.

'Thought someone might have noticed this was missing,' he said, holding up the violin case.

'Oh, thank heavens!' Her face shone with relief. 'I tried to ring you earlier. Where did Millie leave it?'

'In the limo. She was so excited after spending the afternoon playing with that music teacher's daughter, she forgot all about it.'

Jen turned and called back into the house, 'Millicent, come and see what Harry's brought you.' Then she sent a cautious smile his way. 'You look so different when you're not wearing your uniform.'

'Ditto,' he said, trying to sound cool. He'd only seen Jen in the power suits she wore to the office, but at home...with bare feet and wearing pink, for heaven's sake...

He found himself staring at her pale pink stretch trousers and her softly clinging T shirt with rose buds embroidered around a scooped neckline. Her neat, toned body. Soft strands of hair escaped from the casual knot on top of her head.

She looked past him out into the narrow street. 'Where'd you park the limo?'

'Ah—I'm on my bike tonight.'

Her surprised gaze found the gleaming black and silver Harley-Davidson parked in her driveway and she seemed to take a step back as if she were suddenly afraid of him.

'I was just passing,' Harry said quickly. 'I'll be off now. Say hello to Millicent for me.'

Like a puppy responding to its name, Millicent appeared at Jen's side. She took one look at Harry and her violin and leapt forward with an ecstatic squeal.

'My violin!' she shouted, her round eyes almost popping out of her face as she flushed pink with excitement. 'Harry found it!'

As Harry handed it over she hugged it to her chest, like a mother cleaving a lost child to her bosom.

'She treats her violin like a doll,' Jen told him quietly. 'Wraps it in silk and has it lying in its little case beside her bed at night.' Then, to Millicent, she said, 'Don't forget to say thank you to Harry.'

The little girl placed the violin case carefully on the floor and hugged Harry's waist. 'Thank you, thank you, thank you. I love you, Harry.'

Harry reddened as he patted the top of her head. 'That's OK, tiger.' Then, to Jen, he said, 'I'd better be going, then. Catch you later. I'll fetch the Duchess from your office at ten tomorrow for gymnastics, right?'

'That's it,' Jen said, nodding, and then her face pulled into a self-conscious grimace as if she'd thought of something embarrassing. 'Oh—um, afterwards, could you bring her back to Maurice's salon in George Street?'

He frowned. 'He's not trying for more publicity, is he?'

'No. I'm trying to cram a hair appointment into my lunch hour.'

'Oh, oh.' Harry couldn't resist a teasing grin. 'You're going to let that poser wreck perfectly good hair.'

'No,' she responded with exaggerated dignity. 'I'm going to let a recognised genius turn me into something stunning.'

'Yeah, right.' He almost said something stupid then about how surprisingly OK she looked now without Maurice's help, but Millicent was there and the cosy welcome of her house was still getting to him, so he turned and headed for the steps. 'OK. I'm off, then.'

'Don't go, Harry,' a little voice pleaded. 'I want to play my violin for you.'

Struth! Harry hovered on the top step.

'I have to practise for my recital.'

'Recital?' he repeated, shocked. Weren't little girls supposed to spend their days playing with dolls and giving tea parties?

'It's on Sunday afternoon,' Jen explained. 'All the pupils are giving a little concert for their parents.'

'My Mummy is going to come,' Millicent added happily.

'If she can get back in time,' Jen amended, her eyes telegraphing her doubts that her sister would be there.

'But I want to play for you now,' Millicent said. 'Come on, Harry.'

What could he say? There were already so many adults who were too busy to give this poor kid any attention—her father, mother, grandmother, the nanny. He glanced at Jen.

'You're welcome to come in and listen, of course,' she said, looking more uncertain than she sounded.

Listening to a five-year-old scraping horse hair against strings wasn't his idea of a bachelor's night, but what the heck? 'I'd love to hear you,' he told Millicent.

Following them inside was like entering a time warp. Jen's place was even more like his grandmother's house than Harry would have believed possible.

'I inherited this house from an old friend,' Jen said, as if reading his thoughts, as he glanced curiously left and right. 'It's why I came back to Brisbane.'

'You must have made a big impression on him if he left you his house.'

She smiled. 'I'd known Alice since I was very small, when we used to live up the road. I was a Brownie and I was very into lending a hand and doing good turns. I came down here one day to ask Alice what I could do to help her and—' She shrugged. 'We had one of those magic friendships that's hard to explain—where the generation gap makes no difference at all.'

'And you're still doing good turns,' Harry said, thinking of the way her sister had landed Millicent on Jen with little thought for the inconvenience.

'It becomes a habit.'

As she led him through the kitchen his curiosity got the better of him. 'What *is* that smell?'

'Shepherd's pie.'

Of course. The aroma had seemed familiar and yet he hadn't been able to place it. Shepherd's pie had been one of his favourites when he was a kid, but he hadn't eaten it in at least a decade. 'Does it have a mashed potato topping?'

'Yes. It's browning in the oven now.'

'And will you eat it with tomato sauce?'

'Sure. Why?'

'Just curious.'

The homey factor hiked another ten points and Harry felt more uneasy.

Jen took him through to a sunroom that had been created by closing in the long back verandah with windows. 'Alice knew how I felt about this house and she had no family of her own but, just the same, I couldn't believe she left it to me. I've kept everything almost exactly as it's always been—Alice's furniture, her china and silver. I even inherited her cat and her bird.'

'And her garden,' Harry said, walking to the window and looking out into the backyard, which had been terraced into the hillside. The light was almost gone but he could make out staked tomatoes, rows of lettuce and clumps of herbs.

'The garden's a bit of a worry,' Jen admitted, bending to switch off the CD player. 'I love it, but it takes a lot of upkeep. I've only been here a month so I haven't had time to kill too many plants yet, but the weeds are beginning to get away on me.'

As Millicent laid her violin case on a small table and opened it carefully, Jen said in an undertone, 'Take a seat and watch this. You're in for a treat.'

Obediently, he settled into a padded cane chair, but it wasn't necessary to feign interest in Millicent's performance. Even before she began playing the intense concentration on the child's face as she tightened her bow string and lifted the small violin to her shoulder fascinated him. She stood carefully with her feet apart and her shoulders back and took her time positioning the fingers of her left hand on the strings.

She played a simple waltz, frowning as she focused her entire attention on the way she drew the bow back and forth. The music was surprisingly tuneful. No squeaks or scratches. Millicent wasn't Mozart, but she was obviously talented. 'Hey, that was terrific!' Harry cheered, clapping madly as she finished.

'Would you like some more?' the little girl asked, her face glowing from his enthusiasm.

'Why, sure.' He leant towards Jen. 'Did she inherit this talent from your family?'

She laughed. 'Not that I know of. I don't know where it comes from.' Then she slipped out of her seat. 'I'll just check on dinner.'

Millicent played two more pieces while Jen was gone and there were no glaring mistakes that Harry could notice. The most interesting thing was how much the little girl seemed to love playing. Plain little Millicent had been transformed the minute she lifted that fiddle out of its case.

She was born with the music in her, he thought. No one will have to nag Millicent to practise. For her it isn't a chore; it's a vital part of who she is.

In the kitchen Jen turned off the oven and stood in the middle of the room with her hands pressed to her heated cheeks. Having Harry in her house made her far too jittery. She wasn't used to having a man here.

Certainly not a man like him. Even after he'd removed the leather jacket he'd worn on the bike, his black T-shirt and jeans seemed so— so intensely *masculine*.

And now she had to decide whether she should invite him to stay for dinner. But dared she?

She'd come back to Brisbane and this house on impulse after Dominic left her. Alice's bequest had been timely and the home that Jen had always loved had beckoned like a familiar, comforting refuge. Now Harry's presence felt a threat to its cosy peacefulness. Nevertheless, he had been very obliging about Millicent. And he'd seemed so interested in the shepherd's pie, for heaven's sake.

In the next room Millicent stopped playing. If Jen was going to invite him to stay it was now or never. *OK, I'll ask him.* The second the decision was made a tiny glow of anticipation started low inside her, but she tried to ignore it as she went to the doorway and said, 'Dinner's ready.'

Harry jumped to his feet.

'You're very welcome to stay,' she added, knowing that her smile looked self-conscious and cautious.

Millicent sent Harry another pleading look and Jen kept her hands shoved inside oven mitts, trying to act as if she invited men she hardly knew to dinner on a regular basis.

As he glanced from one to the other, a corner of Harry's mouth quirked into an equally awkward smile. 'Ah—thanks, ladies. That shepherd's pie smells really tempting.' Rubbing a hand over the back of his neck, he grimaced. 'But I'll have to take a raincheck on dinner. I've got—ah—plans for this evening.'

Of course he would have plans. Jen swallowed a stupid rush of disappointment as she watched him wave to Millicent and then cross the kitchen and begin to head back down the hall, hurrying as if he couldn't get away fast enough.

'Hope the recital goes well,' he remembered to call back to Millicent.

'I'll take her to her concert on Sunday,' Jen said as she hurried behind him down the hallway.

He paused near the front door.

'I'll probably take my mother, too,' Jen went on, needing to talk, wanting to show him that it didn't bother her in the least that he was in such a hurry to get away. 'The other kids will have so much support from parents and brothers and sisters and grandparents.'

Harry nodded. 'You're very generous with your time.' Then, as he moved through the doorway, he brushed close to her and her heart began to pound. Next minute he was reaching to touch a strand of her hair that had fallen out of its knot.

She froze at his touch, heat rushing into her cheeks.

His grey eyes were breathtakingly close to hers. Too close. 'This straight look is *so* last summer,' he said, mimicking Maurice. His voice lowered to dark chocolate as he let the loose, satiny strand slide between his finger and thumb. '*So* five minutes ago.' Jen's heart

seemed to hurl itself from a very high cliff.
'That guy wouldn't have a clue,' he said.

Then he left, disappearing into the inky
night, leaving Jen clutching the door-post because her knees had given way.

Halfway through eating her shepherd's pie,
Millicent let out a loud sigh.

'That's a big sigh for a little girl,' Jen said.

'I was thinking about Harry and then I felt
sad.'

'Did you, darling? Why?'

'I like Harry.'

'Yes, but why does that make you sad?'

'I was wishing Harry could be my Daddy.'

'Goodness.' Jen gulped, not sure how to respond. 'Has Mummy ever talked to you
about—about your father?'

'Yes.' Millicent gave a very definite nod.
'She told me that she lost him, but one day
she's going to find him again for me.'

Jen tried to swallow the lump in her throat.
'Really?'

'I hope he's as nice as Harry.'

Reaching across the table Jen squeezed Millicent's hand. 'I'm sure he will be.'

Much later, when Millicent was tucked into bed, Jen sat in a pool of lamplight with her legs curled comfortably beneath her and a book unopened on her lap, lost in thought.

She'd tried to read, but her concentration had been shot to pieces, hijacked by thoughts of Harry, of how attractive he was, how he'd made her feel when he'd fiddled with her hair—and how disappointed she'd been when he left.

The silly part was that, although she zinged and zapped whenever he was near, she knew in her bones that Harry Ryder was wrong for her. He was everything she'd always resisted.

Since the beginning of her teens, when boys had suddenly stopped being annoying jerks and had become alarming Potential Boyfriends, she'd shied away from guys like Harry. She'd never felt pretty enough or exciting enough to consider herself equal to his kind of overt masculinity. It came with too much testosterone and danger and she was still as wary now as she had been when she was fourteen... She had learned that she was destined to date the B list—nice safe, unexciting guys.

Not sexy chauffeurs who owned Harley-Davidsons and came wrapped in so much mystery you could tell at first glance they were dangerous.

CHAPTER FOUR

THE next day Jen spent her lunch hour under a forest of aluminium foil strips and blue-coloured bleach. As she sat in Maurice's busy salon and eyed the alarming sight in the mirror she reassured herself that this stolen time was justified. Looking well-groomed and fashionable was important for her self-esteem and, ultimately, her career.

If she wanted to strengthen her career prospects in her boss's absence glamorous hair would give her the morale boost she needed. Better still, it would be an outward sign that she was moving on, getting over Dominic and starting afresh.

Sidestepping Harry.

She closed her eyes, unwilling to see her reflection blush at the thought of Harry Ryder. *Fool.* Despite her best intentions to put him right out of her mind, she'd wasted another night losing vital sleep while she tossed and turned.

A hand patted her arm through the plastic cape and she jumped.

'Oh, Millicent!' she exclaimed, finding her niece beside her. 'My mind was miles away.' She gave the little girl a quick hug. 'How was gym?'

'OK.' Millicent smiled as she looked at the amazing clutter on Jen's head. 'Mummy gets that stuff on her hair, too, but Harry says—'

'*Harry?*' Jen spun around, dismayed. Was Harry here? The last thing she wanted was for him to see her looking like this.

'Are you looking for him?' Millicent asked.

'No, not really.' A flash of fire burnt her cheeks.

'He was going to talk to you,' Millicent said. 'But he decided you were too busy, so he wrote you a note.' She handed Jen a page torn from the back of her notebook. A message was scribbled in a barely legible scrawl.

Hi Jen,
  I've decided I'll join you for Millicent's

recital on Sunday afternoon. She deserves a cheer squad.

   See you then,

   Harry

   PS You're right. Maurice is a genius. That aluminium look is SO next week and it really suits you!

Jen shot Millicent a horrified glance. 'Harry was in here? He saw me like this?'

Millicent nodded and smiled. Jen groaned. *Get over it. His opinions don't matter.* To Millicent she said, 'Harry's going to come to listen to you play the violin on Sunday.'

Millicent smiled. 'Yes, he told me.' Then she looked away quickly and her lip trembled.

'Mills, what's the matter?' Jen touched the little girl's cheek and turned her face so she could see the sadness in her little button eyes. 'Don't you want Harry to come?'

'Yes, I do,' she said. 'But I want Mummy to come, too.'

'I know,' Jen said softly, suppressing a

sigh. 'We'll ring her again tonight and remind her about your recital. You never know, she might be able to make it back in time.'

Jen didn't tell Caro that Harry was coming to the recital. As they drove towards the music teacher's home in Chapel Hill she thought about mentioning it several times, but the words died on her lips when she pictured her mother's reaction.

She could imagine the wide-eyed interest, the oohs and ahs of surprise. Jen loved her Mum, but there were times when Caro's dabbling in her social life became excessive. There was an awful chance that this afternoon could turn into a game of matchmaking once Caro set eyes on Harry again.

She was relieved that they arrived before him.

Millicent's music teacher had converted the ground floor of her home into a studio with large sliding glass doors that opened onto a courtyard. Tubs of fig trees and palms edged the area and it was shaded by vine-covered pergolas. Jen, Caro and Millicent nodded to the carefully dressed children and their parents who were chatting and greeting each other.

Millicent didn't appear at all nervous, but she scanned the guests carefully.

Oh, dear, Jen thought. *She's still looking for Lisa.* They'd rung Perth again yesterday. Lisa had told Millicent that she was terribly sorry but she didn't think she'd be back in time, but the child had still clung to a tiny hope.

I know Lisa's not going to show. The poor kid's going to be so disappointed.

'Oh, my!' Caro said loudly beside her. 'Look who's here.'

Jen turned to see Harry coming round the corner of the house and she forgot to breathe.

Dressed in a white open-necked shirt with the sleeves rolled back to his elbows and charcoal-grey trousers, he crossed the courtyard towards them with slow, confident strides. Tanned skin showed at his throat and on his forearms and his dark curly hair and powerful build made her think of a Roman gladiator.

Several heads turned to watch his approach.

'Darling, your new boyfriend is rather beautiful,' Caro said.

'He is *not* a boyfriend.'

Caro cast a quick appraising glance over Jen's simple sleeveless linen dress in a demure shade of cinnamon. 'Your new hairstyle looks nice but putting a few streaks in your hair isn't enough, Jennifer. You really should wear something a little more eye-catching.'

'I don't plan to catch anyone's eye,' Jen said.

'But you should, dear. You need to make the most of your looks now while you're young and still have them. When I was your age I loved to be daring. I wore bikinis, mini skirts, hot-pants—whatever was the rage.'

As Harry drew close Caro's face broke into a broad smile and Jen muttered out of the side of her mouth, 'Now behave yourself, Mother.'

To her relief Harry was distracted by Millicent. As soon as he greeted them the little girl grabbed his hand and demanded his attention. 'Have you seen my mother?'

His face softened as he looked at her. 'No, kitten,' he said gently. Millicent's face and shoulders drooped and Harry shot a concerned glance Jen's way. She shook her head.

Stepping back quickly, he gave a low whistle. 'But look at our Duchess! Doesn't she look swish?' His smile took in her full-skirted white voile dress with its blue silk sash, her powder-blue shoes and white lace socks. 'Turn around; let me see the back.'

Jen was glad she'd made the effort to drive over to her sister's apartment to hunt for suitable clothes for this afternoon. Millicent giggled and twirled obediently and the disappointment in her eyes faded as Harry's eyes flashed in his admiration of her dress. 'You look gorgeous. You definitely look like a VIV!'

'What's that?' she asked.

'A Very Important Violinist.'

'Is that even better than a duchess?'

'Absolutely.'

Her little button eyes shone.

But then Harry's gaze shifted back to Jen and his face grew serious as he studied her, taking particular interest in her new hairstyle with its sophisticated streaks of silver, ash-blonde and smoke, courtesy of Maurice.

For a moment he looked slightly puzzled but then he turned to Caro, raised a dark eyebrow and said, 'What more could a man ask than to be accompanied by three lovely ladies at once?'

Caro's smile was of the cat with the cream variety.

'Millicent,' she said. 'Why don't you come and introduce me to your music teacher?'

Jen drew in a sharp breath as she watched Caro hurry away with Millicent. Mother's trying to match-make already, she thought, and cast a wary glance back to Harry. He was still looking at her and the expression on his face sent her heartbeats scampering.

'Why are you staring?' she asked, hating the way he could unnerve her so easily.

'You look different,' he said. 'I'm trying to work something out.'

'What on earth do you mean?'

'We haven't met before, have we?'

'Before last Wednesday? Of course not.' She looked away for a moment, forcing herself to calm down. Maybe her wits were scattering like leaves in a gust of wind, but one thing was certain: if she'd met Harry Ryder in the past she would have remembered.

'I didn't think we could have met, because I would have remembered,' he said. 'Maybe I saw your picture in a magazine.'

She frowned at him. 'I very much doubt it.'

'I've just had this strange feeling that I've seen you in something like a wedding photo.'

'It can't have been me,' she told him, desperate that he drop this conversation. Caro would return at any minute and she would sense how flustered Jen was. 'The only wedding I've been to recently was at a place called Mullinjim, way out in the outback.'

He snapped his fingers and grinned broadly. 'That's it. Mullinjim. It was Jonno Rivers's wedding to that lovely girl with the French name.'

'Camille,' Jen supplied, stunned. 'She's my best friend. We worked together at *Girl Talk* magazine in Sydney. But how did you know I was there? Have you been spying on me or something?'

'Spying? No, of course not. I grew up in the Mullinjim district and I've known Jonno all my life.'

'Really?'

'Yes,' he said, grinning. 'Really.'

This is merely a coincidence. It's not fate. No need to get flustered.

After a pause Harry said, 'You were the bridesmaid, weren't you?'

'Good heavens, yes. But I'm surprised you recognise me from that photo.' Her friend, Camille, had chosen the most stunning bridesmaid's dress for her to wear and she'd looked much more glamorous than she usually did. Swift on the heels of that thought came her mother's voice echoing in her head: *What have I been telling you, Jennifer? You need to put more effort into your wardrobe.*

'I tried to get to Jonno's wedding,' Harry said, 'but there was a bit of drama that kept me in the Philippines.'

'The Philippines?' Another surprise. 'Were you chauffeuring there or were you on holiday?'

For a moment she thought she'd caught him out. There was the merest flash of annoyance on Harry's face, but it was so brief she couldn't be sure she hadn't imagined it and his expression was impassive as he said, 'I took a break there last year.'

She waited for him to elaborate but, to her chagrin, he didn't. He simply crossed his arms over his massive chest and continued to grin at her. 'When Jonno sent me the wedding photo I was very sorry I'd missed the wedding.'

Heavens, he's flirting! But that was only because he couldn't help it. Men as drop-dead-sexy-looking as Harry Ryder had flirting genes built into their DNA.

She took a deep breath and tried to look calm and cool as her mother returned with Millicent and Jen was grateful that it was time for everyone to be seated for the recital.

'You were wonderful,' they all reassured Millicent after she'd played her little waltz.

Harry, who was sitting next to Jen, leaned close and whispered, 'You're the best violinist here by a country mile.'

Millicent dimpled briefly, but then she looked swiftly towards the door. Jen saw hope flare in the little girl's eyes and then fade. *Merciful heaven, she's still looking for Lisa.*

None of them could make up for the fact that her mother wasn't there. Jen wondered if Lisa had any idea how much her daughter loved her and needed her. If only Millicent had a father in her life to be there for the kid when Lisa was caught up with work.

As people left their seats to mingle, Jen fetched a glass of white wine for Caro and a fruit juice for herself, while Harry took a giggling Millicent to find some chocolate cake.

'Harry's a very fine style of young man,' Caro said, watching him from across the courtyard.

Jen chose not to comment.

'He's not husband material, of course. Being a chauffeur's not exactly going to keep you in the lap of luxury, is it, dear?'

'That's hardly our business.'

'But he's wonderfully dangerous,' Caro added darkly.

'Why do you say that?' Jen looked sharply at her mother.

Caro sipped her wine. 'Surely even you can sense it, darling?'

'I suppose,' Jen said, trying very hard to sound casual, which wasn't so easy considering she'd sensed something threatening in Harry from the minute she'd first set eyes on him and these days his air of danger kept her in a constant dither.

'It's what makes him so attractive,' said Caro. 'He'd be good experience for you.'

'Mother!'

'Jen, face it. He'd be a huge improvement on Dominic.'

About to deny that, Jen changed her mind. What was the point? Comparing Dom with Harry was like comparing plain cheese sauce with hot Thai chilli. Dom was nice-looking, pleasant and comfortable, but a tad dull. Definitely B List. Never even a hint of danger.

But remembering that was hardly a boost to her ego, not when her relationship with Dominic had plummeted towards a rapid, painful death shortly after Lisa had visited them in Sydney. As usual, her sister had stunned everyone in her path with her vibrant, crystalline beauty and, after meeting her, dull Dom had suddenly decided that Jen was even duller.

'We've got into a rut. I need more excitement,' he'd told her. And, to Jen's astonishment, he'd taken off with a new, exciting woman—someone nine years older than him who had flame-red hair and bright blue eyes, plus three young children.

What did *that* say about Jen?

'Who's that man talking to Harry?' Caro asked.

Jen followed the direction of her mother's gaze. Harry was standing near Millicent, watching as she shared chocolate cake and giggles with another little girl, but he was chatting to a finely built, bespectacled fellow who looked to be in his late thirties. He had light brown hair and a kind face.

'I've no idea who he is,' Jen said.

'He's talking about Millicent,' commented Caro.

Jen gave a scoffing laugh. 'Do you think he's a talent scout?' But when she looked again she saw that Caro was right. The man did seem to be taking an interest in Millicent. He and Harry kept looking her way as they talked. Yes, they were definitely looking at Millicent.

When Harry came back to them she couldn't help asking, 'Who was that man?'

'An English bloke named Michael Wolfe,' Harry told them. 'He was very impressed by Millicent's playing.'

'How exciting,' said Caro.

As they watched, the fellow struck up a conversation with Millicent's teacher.

'Apparently she has a beautiful left hand. Something to do with the way she holds it as she presses the strings,' said Harry.

Jen frowned. *Michael Wolfe?* She had a vague feeling she'd heard the name before, but she couldn't place it. The thought nagged at the edge of her concentration and it took her a moment or two to realise that her mother was speaking.

'You two young people have been so generous, looking after Millicent since Wednesday,' Caro was saying. 'It's time I did something to help. I'll take her home to my place this evening. I'm sure you need a break, Jen. You must have all sorts of things you need to do.'

'Well, yes,' said Jen, recovering quickly from her surprise. 'Tomorrow's going to be horrendous. It would be good to have time this evening to run over my notes for the Fortune Banking AGM and then I have—'

'Heavens, girl, you shouldn't be worrying about work on a Sunday evening,' Caro cried, butting in and then shamelessly batting her eyelashes at Harry. 'Should she, Harry?'

'Er, no. I guess not.'

'Of course you shouldn't, Jen.'

'I don't have much choice. My boss is away. I'm overloaded with work.'

Caro gave a dismissive sniff. 'Being so busy at work is a very good reason for relaxing on the weekend. Now listen, Harry. I'm going to borrow Jen's car and take little Millicent home with me for a lovely supper. You wouldn't mind taking Jen in your car, would you?'

Cringe! Too late, Jen realised that her mother had slipped into matchmaker mode. Harry was suspicious, too. She watched his eyes narrow and saw a barely perceptible silent exchange flash between him and her mother.

'Harry, you came here on your motorbike, didn't you?' Jen asked, her mind sweeping in search of a counter-attack. At his nod she added, 'I couldn't possibly get on a motorbike in this dress and, besides, I don't have a helmet.'

'Oh.' Caro made no attempt to hide her disappointment. 'I don't suppose you carry a spare helmet, do you, Harry?'

His silver-grey glance slid sideways to settle on Jen. 'Matter of fact, I do.'

This time it was Jen's turn to say, 'Oh.' She looked down to the ground, battling a bewildering urge to go with Harry if he offered. It was an urge that surprised the heck out of her. What had happened to her usual choice to be sensible and safe?

'That's settled, then,' Caro said, beaming triumphantly. 'I still have a spare set of your car keys, Jen.' And, before Jen could come to her senses and object, Caro sailed off to collect Millicent, who was playing hide and seek among the potted fig trees and palms with the other budding musicians.

Jen looked towards Harry. 'I'm sorry. I'm afraid my mother can be a bit obvious.'

'Devious is the word I'd choose,' he said with a slow smile.

'Devious *and* obvious,' Jen said and she sighed. 'You know you don't have to take me home.'

'I'd worked that out,' he replied. 'But, as it happens, I'm in a gallant mood.'

'Oh,' Jen said again, thrown completely off-balance by his unexpected reply. 'And I'm supposed to be grateful that you're giving me an opportunity to put my life in your hands?'

'You've never been on the back of a bike?'

'No.'

He frowned. 'Would you be frightened?'

I'd be terrified. Terrified of you and your bike. She shrugged in an attempt to look off-hand. 'I've tried a lot of new things lately. I suppose I should add motorbikes to the list.'

Harry regarded her thoughtfully. His eyes were clear, clear grey. Dominic's were blue, and blue eyes were supposed to be the sexiest, weren't they? Since when had grey become so sexy? 'Everyone should take a ride on a bike at least once in their lives,' he said. 'Be a devil.'

'I guess most girls would be thrilled to have you take them for a ride,' she said.

He merely grinned but after that he took it for granted that she was coming and Jen found herself being led to the footpath and handed a helmet. It felt enormous as she hauled it on.

'We can always disappoint your mother and I can drive you straight home,' Harry said, his teasing smile lingering.

'Don't dream of trying anything else,' she said, but her heart was doing somersaults. He was so unlike any man she'd ever dated and the very thought of being alone with him filled her with a wonderful, terrifying trepidation.

For answer he merely smiled and said, 'Hold tight while I check that your chin strap's secure.'

And because he was so suddenly close, *touching* close, Jen held her breath and didn't say another word. Then he swung a leg over the huge machine and called, 'Hop on.'

It was hard to climb up when her knees were trembling and she had to keep one hand on the hem of her dress.

'Get close to me so you can hang on,' Harry said, grinning at her over his shoulder, but his grin faded as he saw the tension in her face. 'Are you still scared?'

'Just take me home, Harry.'

'No need to worry,' he said more gently. 'I'm even better at riding motorbikes than driving limos. You'll love it once we get going.'

Jen kept her eyes tightly shut as they roared down the busy main road leading from Chapel Hill through Kenmore and she clung to Harry for dear life, but gradually, to her surprise, her fear began to subside.

Being on a bike didn't feel nearly as precarious as she'd expected and she couldn't deny that it was rather thrilling to lean into Harry's leather jacket with her arms wrapped tightly around his waist and her knees gripping his thighs. He felt incredibly muscular and deliciously male and if she concentrated hard she could smell enticing faint traces of his cologne, diluted by fresh air and sunshine.

When they reached Toowong he must have sensed she was feeling braver and he called over his shoulder, 'How about we take a quick trip up Mount Coot-tha to see the view?'

'All right,' she called back, nervous but grimly determined. If she was serious about casting off the Very Nice Jen, the cautious, mousy Jen, she should try to embrace every chance to change.

Gum trees flashed past as they swerved off the busy freeway and took the curving road that climbed to Brisbane's most popular lookout. Within a very few minutes the summer air felt cooler and fresher. Jen caught a whiff of eucalyptus, sharp and tangy, and she spied a bush turkey, its red head and bright yellow wattle a blur of colours as it scurried through the scrub. She'd always loved the pockets of intact, peaceful bushland that could still be found close to the city in Brisbane.

'That was terrific,' she admitted to Harry when they pulled into the parking lot at the top of the hill. 'Thank you.'

'I thought you might like it once you stopped screaming.'

'I was *not* screaming.'

He grinned and she gave his arm a playful slap, then unsnapped her chin strap, removed her helmet and ran her fingers through her hair, shaking it free.

'I like this new look,' Harry said, watching her hair. 'It's lovely.'

His compliment pleased her, but she hoped he couldn't guess how much. 'So you agree that Maurice is a genius?'

'I take back every bad word I said about the man.' He touched a flyaway strand and his smile was slow and exceedingly dangerous. Jen held her breath. Harry was flirting with her and, after three years of monogamy with Dom, her own flirting skills were decidedly rusty. Not that they'd ever been very brilliant.

'Let's check the view,' he said slowly, his watchful grey eyes still lingering on her.

'Yes, let's,' she said, feeling breathless. Rusty flirting skills or not, she recognised hot desire when it consumed her.

After a long pulse-pounding moment Harry looked away and they crossed to the fence that bordered the lookout. When she was little her parents had brought every family visitor to this lookout and she'd come with them many times, but it had been years and years since she'd been up here.

Now the widespread city sprawled before them, a vast vista of tiny rooftops, streets and multi-lane highways, bisected by the winding, sleepy Brisbane River and dotted every so often by clumps of bushland. In the nearer suburbs Jen could make out the purple splashes of flowering jacaranda trees, the white of frangipani and the scarlet of poinciana. To the east a forest of skyscrapers marked the CBD. A succession of bridges spanned the river and on the horizon the waters of Moreton Bay shimmered in a smoky-blue haze.

'Whenever I look at a sweeping view like this I can't help remembering that we're standing on a tiny planet that is hurtling through deepest space,' Harry said.

'Good heavens.' Jen stared at him.

'It's an exhilarating thought, isn't it?'

'Not exhilarating,' she said. 'It's scary.' She hugged her arms.

'Are you cold?'

'No, not cold, just feeling less safe. I can cope with the idea of my world circling the sun, but I don't like to think about an entire galaxy rushing at breakneck speed through the universe.'

'But it's a great thing to think about,' Harry said. 'Here we are, all very busy fussing and fretting over our little lives while our planet is tearing away on an adventure of its own that we'll probably never understand.'

Jen released her breath on a light, jagged laugh. 'So you like speed and danger and mystery?'

'Love it,' he said, smiling at her again. 'I hate to stay in one place for too long.'

That figures. Why did she find his admission depressing? 'No doubt you love thunderclaps and fierce lightning, too?'

'Sure,' he said. 'What about you?'

'I don't mind a storm if I'm safely snug with a roof over my head, but I prefer clear blue skies.'

Harry smiled. 'So you're not a risk-taker?'

'I guess not.' *In other words I haven't actually changed at all. I'm still boring, boring, boring.* 'I suppose you think I'm missing out on a lot.'

'You get a great view when you fly close to the sun.'

'I'll bet,' Jen said. 'But you get burned, too.' She dragged in a deep breath. 'So tell me, does anything frighten Harry Ryder?'

A flicker of surprise disturbed his features. He looked away, but she could see that his expression had tightened and his mouth was strangely grim. When he turned back to her he offered her such an unexpectedly sad smile that Jen's heart skipped a beat. 'I'm not going to tell you,' he said softly. 'But, even if I did, you wouldn't believe me.'

Once again their gazes held and Jen shivered, not because of the cool mountain-top air that whisked and played with her hair, but because she sensed that, even though Harry hadn't actually answered her question, he'd answered something else, something deep and vitally important. Problem was, she had no idea what it could be. It was like receiving a coded message with no clues.

She gave a little shake and told herself she was being fanciful. 'So what *will* you tell me?' she asked.

'About myself?'

'Yes.'

He frowned and his eyes grew wary. 'I'm not going to talk you into a coma about my past relationships.'

'That's OK. I don't want to discuss mine either.'

'So what would you like to know?'

Why are you working as a chauffeur when you're obviously intelligent and could hold down a much more prestigious position? She couldn't ask that for fear of sounding like a snob. 'Tell me about Mullinjim, where you grew up. Were you on a cattle station near Jonno's?'

'No, worse luck. Might have been all right if I'd lived on a property, but I lived in town.' Leaning forward, Harry rested his arms on the lookout's railing. 'My parents own a butcher's shop and that's where we lived, all six of us, behind the shop in the town's main street.'

'You sound as if you didn't like it much.'

'I didn't.' Harry looked out at the view and his face twisted into a wry grimace. 'I was the odd one out in my family. I liked to read. I always had my nose stuck in a book. I desperately wanted to know about the world beyond Mullinjim, but my Dad and brothers thought I was weird. They love the bush and have never wanted anything but an outback lifestyle. They're perfectly content with their lot while I've always been restless.'

Jen could relate to that. She'd always felt very different from Caro and Lisa. They were so into glamour and appearances. At times she'd felt closer to her elderly friend Alice, more at home in her house than she had with her mother and sister.

'And your brothers are still in the bush?'

'Yep. All three of them are still in the Mullinjim district. One is a butcher like my father and the other two are fencing contractors.'

'But you left.'

'Yeah.' He let out the word on a disgruntled sigh. 'I got away as soon as I finished school. Country towns can be very claustrophobic.'

She smiled in sympathy and wished it hadn't been so long since she'd gone through this getting-to-know-you routine. She felt a little lost, fascinated but not sure how far to pry. Had Harry's dreams turned sour? Being a chauffeur for a Brisbane car firm didn't sound like the career choice of a restless adventurer.

'Next question,' Harry said, grinning suddenly. 'Come on, Jen.' He flung his arms wide, as if he were inviting her to land a punch on him. 'Ask away.'

'OK.' When he grinned like that her mind whizzed dizzily. 'Let me see…Can you cook?'

'Almost.'

'Oh, um…I guess you want world peace?'

He threw back his head, laughing. 'For ever.'

'Are you sympathetic to animals?'

'Immensely.'

'Star sign?'

'Scorpio. Had a birthday last week.'

'Happy birthday,' she said, smiling. 'Do you like your job?'

His eyes narrowed and there was the slightest hesitation. 'I'm passionate about it.'

She paused, wanting to ask more but, sensing an unspoken warning in Harry's cautious gaze, she shrugged. 'I give up. That'll do for now.'

'My turn,' he said.

'Nothing too personal,' she warned.

'Of course not. OK, let me see. I know you're a great cook.'

'How do you know that?'

'I smelt your shepherd's pie.'

'Oh, that.' *But you didn't stay to taste it.*

'What's your favourite colour?'

'Crumbs. I don't know. Brown.'

'*Brown?*' he repeated, incredulous. 'That's amazing. I didn't think anybody *liked* brown.'

'I do,' she said huffily. 'I like to wear it.' She ran her hands down the sides of her cinnamon-coloured dress.

He dropped his head to one side and studied her through squinted eyes, a faint smile tugging at the corners of his mouth. 'Actually, I'll eat my words. Those colours really do suit you. Your hair, skin and eye colour are all variations on a theme. You're a brown girl.'

A startled little laugh escaped. 'That's what my father called me. I was his little brown girl and, you know, he always said it as if he was paying me a compliment.'

'I'm sure he was,' Harry said, his voice unexpectedly warm and sympathetic.

For a moment Jen was lost in memory. Her father and she were the quiet, plainer family members. Living in the shadow of her mother and Lisa's bright beauty, they'd shared a special understanding.

'Is your father still alive?' Harry asked.

'No,' she said softly. 'He died three years ago. But, Harry, this is no good. We're breaking the rules and getting personal. New topic please.'

'OK, what's your favourite holiday destination?'

That was easy. 'The beach. Any beach.'

'And your favourite sound?'

Your smooth, deep voice. 'My canary's singing.'

'Why are you afraid of me?'

CHAPTER FIVE

ZAP! Blood rushed to Jen's face. 'I'm not afraid of you.'

If Harry noticed her blush he didn't let on. 'I suspect you're lying, but I'll accept that answer for now.' He smiled slowly and it was a smile that seemed to be sending another message, but again Jen couldn't be sure. 'Seen enough of the view?' he asked.

She nodded.

As they crossed to the bike Jen felt as if she were walking a tightrope. It didn't make sense, but she was suddenly quite sure that she could easily topple head over heels in love with this man. She felt an urgent, unexplainable attraction for Harry Ryder that she'd never felt for Dom or any other male she'd met.

But, of course, there was every chance that this entire afternoon was no more than a trifling amusement for him. A diversion. Harry couldn't be particularly attracted to her or he wouldn't have hurried so quickly away from her house.

He was diverting himself with mild flirtation, and it probably wasn't wise to respond in kind. She sensed that if she let down her guard Harry would almost certainly hurt her, not physically, not even intentionally…but, nevertheless, with devastating results.

Her fears seemed justified minutes later when he took off down Mount Coot-tha at a roaring, cracking pace.

'Harry!' she screamed, clinging to him in terror. 'Slow down!'

'Relax,' he shouted back as the bike careened dangerously low to the bitumen while they wheeled around a curve. 'Live a little!'

To their right the mountain fell away steeply. 'You're shortening my odds.'

'Trust me, Jen!'

'Famous last words!'

She was still breathless when they reached Red Hill and shimmied to a halt in her driveway. 'That was irresponsible,' she told him.

'You loved it.'

'Harry, this time I *was* screaming and you ignored me.'

'They were screams of delight.'

As she removed her helmet Harry dismounted and said easily, 'Let me make up for my sins by being a gentleman and walking you to your door.'

Help. Her entire body vibrated with sudden tension. 'Th—thank you.'

On the verandah he stepped close and his gaze locked on to hers. 'You know, that wedding photo of Jonno's didn't do you justice. It didn't show the difference in your eyes.'

Jen gulped. 'You mean the speck in my left eye?'

He touched the left side of her face and electricity flashed through her body. 'It's a fascinating slice of ginger. It makes you unique.'

His smile was devastating, making her feel unexpectedly special, incredibly feminine. Desiring and desirable. 'I have a copy of the photo inside. Would—would you like to come in?'

The bold invitation was out before she had time for second thoughts, but Harry stood rock still, considering her question. The air between them crackled with a terrible, tangible tension.

Jen was trembling as his hands reached for her shoulders and he leaned in to brush a feather-light kiss over her lips.

His mouth was hot against hers and heat flashed under her skin. Her heart thrummed. He took a lingering, sexy nibble of her lower lip and made a soft sound, a mixture of sexy need and frustrated regret. 'That's not a good idea,' he murmured against her mouth. 'I'm not your type, brown girl.' Then he stepped abruptly away from her. 'I've got to go.'

She tried to speak, but couldn't.

'I'll collect Millicent from your mother's tomorrow,' Harry said.

Jen nodded. Turning quickly to her door, she fumbled for her keys, anxious to get inside before Harry saw her bright red face.

Inside, she sagged against the door, feeling a thousand versions of foolish. How embarrassing! Harry had paid her a compliment about her mismatched eyes and she'd made a quantum leap in her thinking and decided he found her sexy.

She'd invited him inside. How could she have been so carried away? Maybe her hair had been artificially enhanced, but it wasn't enough to turn her into a *femme fatale*. Fool! How could she have forgotten that beneath the hair she was still plain, brown, mousy Jen?

How could she have thought that a sexy bachelor like Harry Ryder might have wanted to come inside with a dormouse?

Nevertheless she felt a puzzling surge of anger at Harry. Marching through the lounge, she snatched up a cushion from the sofa and punched her fist into it. What right had he to flirt with her and send her melting smiles and then dash away as if she'd developed the plague?

The thoughtless, teasing, insensitive, egotistical brute.

In the kitchen she stopped and took a deep breath. She had to calm down. This much anger was unhealthy. Ridiculous, really. Wasn't this what she wanted? No Millicent and a long, empty, distraction-free Sunday evening to go over her notes. Now she had yards and yards of free time and she could get to know the Fortune company's annual report inside out. Backwards.

Forget Harry.

She went on to her study, unzipped her briefcase, pulled out the Fortune folder and tried to assure herself that by tomorrow morning she'd be grateful that Harry hadn't stayed.

Next morning, Gerald Harvison, Chairman of Fortune Banking Corporation, was a mass of nerves, but Jen was calm. Determinedly calm. Calm as an iceberg and so immaculately groomed she looked like a corporate version of superwoman.

Last night, after she'd prepared her notes, she'd washed and blow-dried her hair, filed and buffed her nails, ironed her white linen shirt and brushed minute specks from her dark suit.

There was nothing like keeping busy to get over a stupid, embarrassing *faux pas*.

Now she flashed Gerald Harvison a bright, stainless-steel smile and took him on a tour of the AGM's venue so he could admire the corporate imaging and branding she'd organised. The sight of his company's logo on the walls and on the speaker's lectern, as well as a huge screen above the official table, seemed to calm him and, after she'd taken him through fifteen minutes of pre-conference briefing, he was looking and sounding more like a conqueror.

After that Jen wasn't particularly surprised when he delivered the executive summary without a stumble and managed to convince everyone, press included, that the company was in a sound financial position.

Afterwards he thanked Jen profusely, but her mind was already flying ahead to the next job. She had to keep herself busy so she didn't think about *him*—He Who'd Rejected Her.

Thank heavens for the pressure of too much work. It was a girl's saviour. At the very least it stopped her from noticing that her insides seemed to be falling to bits.

OK, next stop was the launch at Lawson's Bookstore. She had to be there by midday to make sure the drinks and nibbles she'd ordered were in place and everything was ready to go. And she needed to ascertain whether the book's author needed his hand held as well.

As her taxi took her south across the Brisbane River via the William Jolly Bridge, she scanned the press release she'd put together, refreshing her memory about Taggart. A former 'A grade' Rugby player…well travelled, choosing more often than not to visit the world's trouble spots… He didn't sound particularly literary.

And he mustn't be much of a looker. There was no photo in any of the publicity she'd received. But apparently his stories were very popular, especially with male readers. Gory blockbusters were not Jen's cup of tea, so she really knew very little about him. She hoped he wouldn't expect her to.

She scanned the notes. 'A man who lives without a safety net,' his publishers claimed. 'Taggart walks on the dark side and this is reflected in his gripping writing, where the lines between good and evil are invariably blurred.'

She hoped those tendencies didn't spill over into his public behaviour. She needed old H R to be charming and diplomatic in his handling of the press. The last thing she wanted was a repeat of last week's experience with Maurice.

The traffic was heavy and by the time she arrived at Lawson's in Brisbane's trendy West End several journalists and their entourage were already there and tucking into the food.

Close by the catering table the booksellers had arranged a stunning display—a huge mountain of H R Taggart's latest book, *Dead Certainty* and, behind it, enormous posters displaying the glossy black cover, decorated with bloodstained dice and the author's name in blood red.

Taggart had plenty of support from his publisher and he'd already produced a string of books so, with luck, this press conference would be a breeze.

Jen checked her watch. The classy bookstore was filling rapidly now. The only thing missing was the vital H R Taggart himself.

'I haven't met this author,' she confided to one of the sales assistants, after glancing anxiously at her watch for the third time. 'I've only dealt with the publishers. Is Taggart likely to be late? Is he the absent-minded type?'

'Oh, no,' the woman said warmly. 'Far from it. He's—' She paused as the babble of conversation in the shop diminished suddenly and Jen glanced towards the door.

'No!' Her stomach dropped to her toes and she lost all interest in Taggart.

Harry was strolling into the shop with Millicent in tow.

Her first reaction was to blush fiercely, but that was swiftly overtaken by righteous dismay. Good grief! What could have gone wrong this time? What was he doing *here*?

Harry was supposed to have picked Millicent up from Caro's forty minutes ago and taken her to her swimming lesson. She rushed forward before he could draw too much attention to himself. 'I'm sorry, Harry, but there's an important author about to be interviewed here.'

She felt a stab of panic. There was something wrong with the way Harry looked. 'What's the matter?' she demanded. 'Why isn't Millicent at swimming?'

'Apparently the pool's required for a high school swimming carnival today and the Junior Aquanauts have been cancelled.'

'*So?*'

He ruffled the top of Millicent's head and the little girl smiled up at him with round, trusting eyes. 'So I had to bring the Duchess with me.'

'For Pete's sake, Harry, I accept that a cancelled class could pose a slight problem for you, but couldn't you have taken her for a ride? Buy her an ice cream, a hamburger. Anything. I'm sorry, you can't stay here.'

Grabbing his elbow, she tried to push him back through the doorway. It might have been easier to try to push Mount Coot-tha. Harry wasn't budging. She felt an overpowering urge to grab him by the earlobe and haul him outside the way her grade three teacher had evicted countless naughty boys.

'Hold on, Jen,' he said. 'I need to explain something.'

'Not now, Harry.' With both hands she gave his massive shoulder a shove. 'Outside, please. I've got an important function happening here. A VIP author's due any minute.'

'But, Jen!'

How annoying could this man get? Why wouldn't he budge? She wanted to kick him, but that would draw too much attention. Instead she shoved her knee hard against his leg.

'*What do you think you're doing?*'

An enraged voice and a sharp rap on her shoulder brought Jen swinging round to see the furious face of Doug Lawson, the bookstore's proprietor.

'Oh, I'm very sorry about this, Mr Lawson,' she said, giving Harry's shoulder an extra hard thump. 'It's just a personal matter. I'll have it all sorted out in a few seconds. *Outside*, Harry.'

Why was he being so slow about this? Harry was usually surprisingly quick on the uptake. *Especially when he was getting out of her house.*

'Outside?' the proprietor roared at her, pulling on her arm. 'You're sending this man *outside*? Are you out of your tiny mind, lady?' He flashed an apologetic grimace Harry's way. 'Harry, please, come in. I'm so sorry about this—this misunderstanding.' He glared at Jen with excessive dark malice.

Jen frowned at Doug's hand gripping her arm with bruising force and at Harry still refusing to move out of the store and she felt her blood drain to her toes as she shot from clueless to clued-up in one split second.

Everyone in the store was smiling at Harry. On top of that a sudden light bulb moment told her what was wrong with his appearance. Instead of his chauffeur's uniform he was dressed in designer jeans and a white T-shirt. A soft brown leather jacket was slung over his shoulder. Most people Jen knew had to negotiate a small bank loan to purchase that deceptively casual elegance. There was an earring in his left ear. *An earring?*

Oh…my…God…

Her mouth fell open. 'You can't be—?' She gasped as her knees began to shake. 'You're not—?'

But he didn't need to answer. The people milling around him were evidence enough. Harry Ryder was H R Taggart.

Shock rooted Jen to the floor and she stood with her hand pressed against her pounding heart as she watched Harry greet the press and his admiring fans with the practised charm of a superstar.

This was crazy. Harry was a chauffeur. She felt as if she were choking.

'What kind of PR consultant are you?' Doug Lawson hissed in her ear. 'Believe me, I'll be reporting you to your agency. I've never seen such inappropriate behaviour.'

'But I—' she began lamely, then paused. What on earth could she say? *The man's an impostor. He's not a writer's toenail—he's a chauffeur!*

She sniffed back the threat of tears. Tears of embarrassment and anger. A hand touched her elbow. Harry's. She jerked away from him as he tried to lean close. 'Sorry, Jen. I'll explain later.'

'You bet you will.'

'I didn't know you'd be here on this job.'

'But you knew you were a best-selling author. You could have remembered to mention that at some stage in the past week, couldn't you?'

'No,' he said firmly, his lips closing over the word.

'*No*?' Jen was so full of steam she expected to explode on the spot.

'I told you I'll explain later.' He cast an impatient glance to the waiting circle of book-sellers and journalists and Jen held her lips tightly shut, fully aware that on this occasion she was the one creating the scene. Just the same she couldn't help hissing, 'What's with the earring?'

He grinned cheekily. 'The media people always love it. Now listen. Millicent should sit with you while I deal with this lot.'

Despite her confusion she must have nodded because he left her then, carried away on a tide of adoration to pose beside his mountain of books.

The rodent! Not only had he made a fool of her, he was wowing the crowd and showing her how superfluous she was. The last thing H R Taggart needed was a PR consultant to hold his hand while he dealt with the press.

He was a media tart.

And Jen was left to recover from shock and to brood on the sidelines, clinging to the vain hope that she was suffering from hallucinations. Perhaps none of this was really happening.

Fat chance.

She looked down at Millicent. The child was accepting Harry's transformation with her usual calm aplomb. She drank the orange juice Jen fetched for her and munched quietly on crackers and cheese as if there was nothing at all unusual about her chauffeur morphing into a best-selling novelist.

Then again, Jen rationalised, Millicent was used to daily transformations. The girl's mother was a model who spent half her life relaxing around the house in an ancient oversized T-shirt and denim cut-offs and the other half glammed to the max and dripping in jewels like a princess.

Jen glanced one more time in Harry's direction, but he was totally absorbed with his audience. Well, she had more important things to do than sit around like a useless appendage.

'Hey, Mills,' she said. 'Harry doesn't need us and I need a lunch break. Let's get out of here.'

*   *   *

That evening Caro seemed to have been struck by a newfound urge to be grandmotherly and she insisted on taking Millicent again. With the house to herself, Jen phoned her friend Camille, the bride in the famous photo Harry had feigned so much interest in. When they'd worked together in Sydney, she and Camille had shared many long, heart-to-heart deep and meaningfuls. Today she just wanted some hard facts about Harry Ryder.

'Jonno has a whole shelf full of H R Taggart books,' Camille said. 'I'll ask him what he knows.'

Jen could hear Camille repeating her question to her husband, then she came back on the line. 'Jonno knows Harry all right. He and his brother, Gabe, went to school with him. He's still laughing and said to tell you if you've taken up with him make sure you fasten your seat belt.'

'I haven't *taken up* with him,' Jen said, her stomach churning. 'It's just that he's moonlighting as a chauffeur. I'm minding my niece while my sister's away and Harry's been do-ing the driving.'

'Are you worried about Millie's safety?' Camille asked.

'No, nothing like that,' Jen said hastily. 'He's been very good to her. I guess I'm just—um—' Heck, what excuse could she give? 'I'm just curious,' she finished lamely.

She heard Camille pass the news on to Jonno and then heard her say, 'Jonno, be se-rious. What else can I tell her?' There were chuckles in the background and then Camille said, 'I can't get any sense out of him. He advises you to wind down the window and enjoy the ride.'

'Thanks a million,' Jen muttered. She wasn't sure what she'd hoped to learn about Harry, but Jonno's reaction wasn't cheering her at all.

'Hmm,' Camille said. 'I take it this Harry is a hot item.'

Jen was about to remark that he was a sneaking impostor but, not wanting to preju-dice the witness, she held her tongue.

'My dear Jen, if you've gone silent on me that can only mean one thing. You're smitten. Wait till I see what else I can get out of Jonno.' Camille left the phone but Jen could still hear her speaking. 'Jonno, be serious. I need something useful I can tell Jen about this Harry.'

Jonno's voice sounded close to the phone. 'Tell her not to get in the back seat with him.' This was followed by a reprimand from Camille and more masculine chuckles.

Jen cringed. Strike a light! What kind of reputation did the man have?

'Sorry, that's all I'm going to get out of him today,' Camille said. 'I must say I'm intrigued. This Harry of yours sounds—er—fascinating.'

'He's not mine,' Jen said weakly. 'Forget him.'

Jen said goodbye to Camille but, as she replaced the receiver, she heard the throaty roar of a motorbike outside and hot and cold chills chased up and down her spine.

Her stomach churned as she stood listening to the steady footsteps that came up her front path, up the steps, across the wooden verandah, and then the sharp, confident knock on her front door.

CHAPTER SIX

HARRY held his breath as Jen opened her door a bare six inches and glared at him. He offered a smile. 'I was hoping I could speak to you,' he said and he held up a bottle of wine—a fine, chilled Chardonnay.

'You've got a cheek,' she snapped and her eyes snapped with anger too.

'Listen, can I come in? I want to apologise.'

'You're not half as sorry as I am,' she said, keeping a firm grip on the door handle. 'I don't appreciate being conned. That's what you are, Harry Ryder. A con man.'

Damn it, he'd sensed at the bookstore that she was mad at him, but when he'd looked for her at the end of the press conference she and Millicent had vanished.

'Steady on, Jen. I was going to explain but you took off from Lawson's before I had a chance.'

She crossed her arms over her chest. 'Explain away.'

'Can I come inside?'

'I don't think so.'

Harry shot a swift glance back over his shoulder. Across the street a curtain twitched.

'I'm not worried about what the neighbours might think,' she said. 'Just say what you've got to and then leave.'

He felt a surge of righteous anger. Hell, he'd gone out of his way to help this woman and her family over the past week. For thanks she got nasty just because he didn't share every private detail of his life.

'I've come to have a civilised conversation,' he said evenly. 'You can't hold me up on your doorstep like I've committed a capital offence.'

She frowned and her brown eyes grew worried as she considered his words.

'Believe me, Jen, you're overreacting.'

A resigned sigh escaped as she stepped back. 'Five minutes,' she said. 'You should be able to explain everything in less than five minutes.'

She led him into her pretty, old-fashioned lounge, with its faded floral furnishings, and she sat very primly on an upholstered arm-chair. Harry chose the sofa opposite her and he set the bottle of wine on a crocheted doily on the coffee table between them.

'Is Millicent asleep?' he asked.

'She's still at my mother's.' Jen looked up-set, as if she wished she hadn't admitted that, as if she didn't want him to know they were alone. 'I think Mum's planning to ring you in the morning, but she's decided to take care of Millicent for the next couple of days to give me a—a break. So fire away,' she said with businesslike abruptness. 'Why didn't you tell me you were H R Taggart?'

Harry released his breath on a sigh. 'I've made it a rule to only tell people who need to know,' he said. 'My agent didn't mention which PR company had been hired to organise the launch today. All I knew was I had to turn up at Lawson's, so I'm afraid you weren't on my need-to-know list.'

Jen's chin jutted forward. 'But what about—what about—?' She blinked. 'Why didn't you tell me yesterday?'

He leaned forward, resting his elbows on his knees and steepling his hands, fingertips pressed under his jaw as he sought the right words. 'I wasn't ready to.'

'Hello? You were ready to discuss everything from the nature of the universe to your star sign, but not to tell me who you really are?'

I'm afraid that's it in a nutshell.

Harry looked steadily at a spot on the carpet in front of him. Jen had a point. He'd held back on her. Maybe Polly had a point. His grandmother always claimed he was reckless in his treatment of women.

'Look, I didn't go out of my way to stay incognito,' he said at last. 'But I don't run around broadcasting who I am either. I've found that many people change when they find out I'm an author. They either back right off or throw themselves at me but, either way, they're not themselves any more. I hate that.'

Her expression grew pensive as she thought this over.

Trying to lighten the moment, he said, 'I guess they're scared they're going to end up in one of my books.'

'And as you murder so many of your characters, that might not be very flattering.'

'Exactly.' Harry risked a smile and thought he glimpsed an answering glimmer in Jen's eyes.

'I suppose your explanation makes sense,' she said, sighing. 'But what doesn't make sense is the fact that you're working as a chauffeur when you're such a hotshot best-selling author.'

'That's easy to explain. I do it for research.'

'For your books?'

He shrugged. 'What else? I take on all kinds of different jobs. Before I started my current book I spent time working in a bar in the Philippines. Before that I took a job on an oil rig off the north west coast. I like getting the feel of different places and lifestyles. I need to experience interesting variations in human behaviour firsthand.'

Jen eyed him shrewdly. 'And, from what I've been told, it seems the women in your life are research, too?'

'For pity's sake!' That was the kind of joke his mates made, but he didn't want to hear it from her.

'Or do women only rate as bullet points on your own personal hit list?'

'Jen!' Harry leapt to his feet, not sure why he felt so angry, afraid it was because her accusations were too close to the truth for comfort. 'Don't play the shrew. It doesn't suit you.'

'Shrew?' She looked as if she could hardly believe her ears. Flashing a glance at her watch, she rose from her chair with icy dignity. 'Your five minutes are up, H R Taggart.'

Harry sighed. 'Why are you making such a big deal about this? So, you've found out I'm not a full-time limo driver, I'm a writer. What's the problem?'

Instead of heading for the door, he took a step closer to her. 'Just now you said ''from what I've been told''. Has someone been giving you bad press about me?'

She jerked her gaze away from his. 'Just go now, please.'

His eyes narrowed shrewdly. 'That's it, isn't it? You've rung Mullinjim. You've contacted Jonno for some hot gossip about Harry Ryder.'

'I spoke to Camille—and her husband.'

Harry grinned and a throaty chuckle erupted. 'Jonno Rivers? Talk about the pot calling the kettle black! The Rivers boys were the biggest larrikins in the west in their youth. Don't tell me you let Jonno give me a character reference? It's a wonder you haven't had me arrested. What did he say?'

Her expression looked pained.

'Jen?'

'I don't know,' she cried angrily. 'Jonno— he— Oh, heck, he warned me not to get into the back seat with you.'

Harry felt his smile fade. Was his reputation really that bad? He glanced at the unopened bottle of wine on the coffee table and considered the complicated mishmash of feelings that had sent him hightailing it to Jen's this evening.

While he hadn't come with any clear-cut intentions, he couldn't deny that Harry Ryder alone with a woman and a bottle of wine was The Guy Most Likely to…

Down boy! Heel! Perhaps Jonno had inadvertently rescued him from making a serious mistake.

'Well,' he said, after some time. 'Jonno has given you some very good advice.'

'Has he?' she whispered and then she blushed as if she were appalled by her own curiosity.

Harry glanced away. What was Jen asking? Didn't a homemaking Very Nice Girl know better than to ask a man a question like that? 'Would you like to find out, Jen? Do you want to give me a try?'

'No,' she cried vehemently and she turned a horrified shade of beetroot. 'I have no intention— I—'

He began to walk around the coffee table towards her and she watched his approach in a kind of horror-struck daze. No doubt she expected him to haul her into his arms and kiss her senseless. Hell, it was a tempting thought. Damn tempting.

Holding her breath, she stood as stiffly as a hypnotised mouse awaiting the strike of a cobra.

'You're quite safe, Jen,' he said when he reached her. 'I'm not going to ravish you.'

Her mouth opened and shut. She looked mortified. 'Of course you're not,' she said, her voice tight with agitation. 'I know that.'

He reached into his hip pocket and pulled out a folded piece of newspaper. 'But before you chase me away, have you seen today's *Courier Mail*?'

'No.' Her anxious eyes watched his hands as he opened out the page. 'Today's been so—

so hectic I haven't had time to check the papers.'

'Take a look at this.' He gave her the cutting, which included a photo of a man seated at a grand piano and carried the caption *King of the Classical Keyboard.*

'Goodness, it's the fellow who was so interested in Millicent, isn't it?' she said. 'The man at the recital yesterday. What was his name again?'

'Michael Wolfe. Apparently, he's here to play a Rachmaninov piano concerto with the Queensland Orchestra.'

Her eyes grew wide and thoughtful as she stared at the photo.

'It's exciting to think that someone of that calibre thought Millicent showed talent,' Harry said.

She nodded, staring at the picture intently. 'Perhaps he has a personal interest in her.'

'A *personal* interest? Why should he?' Harry frowned. Jen looked as if she knew more than she was letting on.

'No reason, I guess,' she said quickly, as if she wished she hadn't voiced her thoughts aloud. She tapped the page with a forefinger. 'This is very interesting. Can I keep the cutting?'

'Sure.'

She seemed lost in thought and chewed at her lower lip as she tucked the piece of newspaper into her pocket.

Harry drew in a deep breath and tried to ignore the pink fullness of the lip she was worrying. 'Well,' he said. 'I've covered everything I wanted to say, so I guess I'd better be off.'

'Yes.'

But he didn't move.

He stood watching her without speaking, overcome by a sudden reluctance to leave, realising now, when he should go, that he'd been fighting an inner battle all evening. He'd been trying to ignore the relentless drag of his senses. He wanted Jen.

There was something about her—something that transcended mere prettiness, something warm and womanly, soft and touchable. Something good. He felt gripped by a need that went deeper than basic earthy lust. It was as if he had a hurt that would be healed by Jen's touch.

For a full five seconds neither of them moved...then six...seven seconds...eight...nine...ten...

Looking at Jen, being this close to her, was like hearing a teasing scrap of a mysterious, haunting melody without catching the whole tune. He needed to touch her, to taste her. She'd been troubling him for days now. He needed to run his hands through her new silky hairdo, to taste more of her lovely, inviting mouth, to discover more of her soft, smooth skin, to feel every inch of her sweet curves moulded tight against him. He wanted her so badly he was shaking. *Aching*.

She kept her eyes prudently downcast, staring at a worn spot on the carpet.

'Jen, look at me.'

His blood pounded as she slowly lifted her face.

'That's better,' he said hoarsely, but for the life of him he couldn't smile as he reached to cup her chin with his hand. She quivered as his thumb caressed her skin just out of reach of that tempting lower lip. 'We're not still fighting, are we? What say we call a truce?'

Her gaze locked with his. He could sense her confusion. She wanted to trust him, wanted *him*?

He could show her he was trustworthy...

Trustworthy?

Who was he trying to kid? In a matter of days he'd be gone.

Sickeningly painful common sense returned and his hand slapped to his side. 'Damn,' he muttered. 'Jonno's right. You'd be crazy to get into the back seat with me.'

Her mouth fell open with shock. 'I—I—what do you mean?'

'I mean I was on the brink of trying to persuade you to do just that,' he said and he released an awkward, self-mocking chuckle.

'To—to have sex with you?' Her brown eyes seemed huge as he looked at her.

'It was a bad idea.'

'Was it?'

Their eyes locked and her question hung in the air between them like a thin, pulsing thread that could bind them or snap in two. Harry held his breath and his heartbeats thundered in his ears.

She's trusting you! Don't hurt her. 'We don't want things to get complicated,' he said.

'No,' she mouthed, her voice not quite a whisper.

He touched his fingers to hers. 'That's my problem, Jen. With a girl like you, it would be complicated.'

'I know, I know.' Her fingers curled away from his touch and there was bitterness in her voice.

Harry felt stricken. 'I meant that as a compliment. Please believe me.'

'Harry,' she cried, squeezing her eyes shut, as if to ward off the embarrassment of tears. 'Why didn't you leave when your five minutes were up?'

She kept her eyes closed as he stood staring at her. 'Are you OK, Jen?'

'I'm fine. Just go, Harry. Please.'

For far too long he stayed there, knowing that anything he did or said would only make matters worse.

'Good night, then,' he said at last and, as abruptly as the other times he'd left her, he turned and headed quickly for her front door.

CHAPTER SEVEN

LITTLE pearl studs or silver hoops?

The next evening Jen stood in front of her bedroom mirror and studied her reflection as she tried to decide which earrings would go best with her upswept hairdo and navy silk sheath.

Lifting a pearl earring to her left ear and a silver hoop to her right she held them in place and turned her head from side to side, trying to gauge which would look more chic. Perhaps the hoops…

Her phone rang in the kitchen and the earrings clattered on to the glass tray on her dressing table. All afternoon she'd jumped at every phone call, fearing, hardly hoping, but almost expecting that it would be Harry.

She dashed to answer it. 'Hello,' she gasped.

'Jen, dear.'

'Oh, Mum, hi.' Sinking on to a kitchen stool, she tried to calm her breathing and hoped she hadn't sounded too disappointed that her mother wasn't Harry.

'I was wondering if you'd heard from Lisa,' Caro said. 'Did you know she's back in Brisbane?'

'No. When did she arrive?'

'She flew in at midday.'

'How is she?'

'She's fine, I think. She didn't have much to say. You know what Lisa's like, always in a hurry. I organised for Harry to deliver Millicent straight to her place.'

Jen's breath caught at the mere mention of Harry's name. 'Mills will be so happy to have Lisa home.'

'And it means you'll be able to get back to normal. By the way, I'm sure Lisa will ring you as soon as she is settled, but she asked me to pass on her thanks. Now, do you have anything nice planned for this evening?'

'Actually, I'm going to a concert.'

'How lovely. Which one?'

'The Queensland Orchestra. The fellow who was so interested in Millicent at her recital is playing a piano concerto.'

She didn't add that her purpose in attending the concert was to get to the Green Room after the performance. With luck, her old press pass from her previous job would secure her access to the area where the musicians entertained VIP patrons. It was a little nosy of her, but she'd decided to meet this Michael Wolfe and pose a few discreet questions.

She'd been struck by the amazing possibility that he could be Millicent's father.

Six years ago Lisa had been madly in love with a musician. It had all happened overseas—somewhere in Europe. Jen had never known the full story. She and Caro had been hurt that Lisa hadn't confided in them.

Her sister had come home, tight-lipped, dispirited and pregnant, and had grimly set about hanging on to her career while building her life as an independent, single mother. There'd been speculation in the press but, after dogged silence from Lisa, the subject had died.

But, ever since Harry had shown her the clipping last night, the more Jen had thought about it, the more she was convinced that Michael Wolfe was Millicent's father. She didn't know what she could achieve by meeting him, so she decided to keep quiet for now, but at least it was a start.

'Are you wearing something eye-catching?' Caro asked.

'I'm wearing my navy silk. I'm going to a symphony orchestra concert, Mother, not a night club. I want to look conservative and cultured.'

'But darling, that's how you always look. You should make yourself more exciting, especially if you're going with Harry.'

'I'm not,' she said, and tried to tamp down a fresh spurt of misery.

'Oh, well...' There was an annoying pause on the other end of the line. 'I was getting such nice vibes about you and that man. You will be seeing more of him even though Millicent's gone home, won't you?'

'I doubt it,' Jen said, forcing a tremor out of her voice. 'There's no reason why I should.' She'd spent the past twenty-four hours coming to terms with the bitter truth that, while Harry Ryder might be a threat to the virtue of just about every female in the universe, he found her exceptionally easy to walk away from.

The sexy beast had no interest in the dor-mouse. She knew she should feel relieved and it was galling to find that she was still upset.

At least her new interest in finding Millicent's father gave her a reason to distract her thoughts elsewhere. 'Mum, I've got to run. 'Bye.'

'Goodbye, Jen. Have a nice evening,' her mother said, sounding as if she thought that was highly unlikely.

In the theatre's foyer Jen bought a programme and stood back from the buzzing crowd as she scanned it quickly, searching for information about Michael Wolfe. She learned that he was thirty-six years old and that he was a masterful pianist who'd studied at the London School of Music and performed all over Europe and in Carnegie Hall in America.

The programme notes claimed he had a massive technique...a splendid feeling for the music of Rachmaninov... His playing was both exuberant and poetic...hinting at unreachable heights of passion.

It didn't surprise Jen that Lisa could have fallen in love with such a gifted man. Although Wolfe wasn't the tall, dark and dangerous kind of handsome most people expected her beautiful sister to go for, there was something understandably sexy and attractive about formidable talent.

As the people in the foyer sipped champagne, chatted and flashed their jewellery, Jen paid scant attention.

She stood quietly in a corner, thinking about Lisa's situation. She'd decided against phoning to tell her sister about tonight's concert. Her guess that Michael Wolfe was Lisa's old flame was really no more than a hunch.

Now she turned her thoughts to the questions she hoped to put to the pianist when she cornered him in the Green Room after the show. Subtlety would be the key. Her main purpose was simply to find out if the musician had ever met Lisa…

A rustle of whispers distracted her and she became aware of a number of heads all turning in the same direction. Mildly curious, she followed the direction of their gazes to see what was causing the stir.

Her blood froze in her veins.

Everyone seemed to be looking at two tall, elegantly handsome figures. Male and female.

Harry Ryder. And her sister.

Together. Arm in arm.

Her heart felt like a clockwork toy gone haywire. How could this be? Lisa had only flown in from Perth at lunch time and—

She backed away as if retreating from a bushfire's blast.

How could Harry Ryder drive Millicent home and now, a few hours later, be an item with Lisa?

It was crazy.

A crush of people swarmed around them but, by standing on tiptoes, Jen could see enough to gauge how spectacular the couple looked. Harry was dashing in a black tuxedo and Lisa looked stunning in golden satin.

Beneath the bright lights Lisa's auburn hair gleamed, her deep green eyes sparkled and her translucent complexion glowed like the marble on a Grecian statue. The impact of her loveliness hit Jen like a sharp, painful smack in the face.

Her old enemy, jealousy, curled nastily in her stomach. She looked down at her own drab navy silk dress. She'd never felt more unbearably conscious of her mousy ordinariness compared with her sister's outstanding beauty.

Lights were flashing around the couple.

Photographers needing images of theatregoers for the society pages fell over each other to get shots of the H R Taggart-Lisa Summers combination.

Retreating through the crowd, Jen trembled as she watched Harry and her sister beam and smile for the cameras. Lisa's gold dress was exquisite—tight, strapless and, no doubt, hideously expensive. Harry's hand was resting on her bare shoulder.

Acid burned in Jen's stomach as Lisa leant close to Harry and more or less nuzzled his neck, whispering something. Harry flashed her one of his gorgeous, to-die-for grins and kissed her.

Kissed her sister! In front of all these people!

Locked his beautiful mouth on Lisa's.

Jen shoved a fist over her own mouth to hold back a cry of dismay. Any plan to attract the celebrity couple's attention, to greet them calmly and find out what was going on, died a swift death.

Maybe she was a prize wimp, but that kiss stole her courage. She couldn't face Harry right now. She had to get away before she made a fool of herself.

It was too bad about Michael Wolfe, but she'd suddenly lost all interest in meeting him. All she wanted was to disappear into the night before either her sister or Harry saw her. Anyway, there was a very good chance that Lisa didn't care two hoots about Michael now that she had Harry in her sights.

Jen's heels beat a frantic tattoo as she hurried down the steps leading from the theatre and into the underground car park where she'd left her car.

Wrenching the car door open, she threw herself into the driver's seat and let her head fall against her hands as she clutched the steering wheel.

She had no claim on Harry. She knew that. And yet...and yet he'd stolen her heart anyway.

What a loser she was. This scenario was a teenage crush and Dominic all over again—the pathetic story of her life. Nothing had changed. She was almost thirty and still living out the same drop-kick patterns that had started in her teenage years. There was always someone prettier, more colourful and exciting to entice guys away from her.

Why, oh why, couldn't Lisa have stayed in Perth?

Next morning Jen dragged herself into the office at eight a.m. after the worst sleepless night of her life. Her head was aching and she was balancing a mug of coffee in one hand and a pile of folders in the other and her phone was ringing way too loudly.

Wincing at the bell's shrillness, she set her coffee on the desk and lifted the receiver. 'Public Persona, Jen Summers.'

'Jen.' It was Sandi from Sydney HQ. 'I'm afraid I have some bad news for you.'

Oh, great! Just what she needed. 'This must be bad news week,' she said, easing into the chair behind her desk. 'I've already had my quota of bad news and it's only Wednesday. You'd better give this to me gently, Sandi.'

'Gently? Ah…well…'

Jen sighed as she dragged her take-away coffee cup across the desk towards her, lifted the plastic lid and drew in a breath of aromatic steam. 'What's the worst you can tell me? I'm not fired, am I?'

'Almost.'

Coffee spilled on to the papers in front of Jen. 'Jeez, Sandi, I was joking. Tell me you're joking, too.' Anger rushed through her like a sky rocket. How could they take this job from her? 'You can't be thinking of firing me. You know I've been working my socks off. I've done a great job.'

'I'm afraid we've received a strongly worded complaint from Eagle and Browne, the publishers who put up the money for that book launch on Monday.'

'Oh.' Jen's headache throbbed harder. She felt ill. 'I take it they've been talking to Doug Lawson from the bookstore.'

'Exactly and they are *not* amused. This author you attacked—'

'I didn't attack him.'

'Apparently that's debatable, Jen. Anyhow, H R Taggart is one of their stars. They're super-sensitive about him. Very protective.'

Big deal.

'In fact, they're so touchy they're threatening to close their publicity account with us. How could you be so unprofessional, Jen? How could you have been so rude to a VIP client?'

'I didn't know he was a client,' Jen said. 'It's—it's a long story.'

'Shorten it.'

Oh, boy. She reached for her handbag and felt inside it, searching for an aspirin. 'I'd already met this—this H R Taggart guy before Monday, but he never told me he was an author, so when he turned up at Lawson's Bookstore I thought he was gate-crashing and—' Jen sighed and squeezed her eyes tightly shut. It all sounded so lame when she tried to explain. 'And so, naturally, I did my best to send him away.'

'By yelling at him and trying to shove him through the door while pummelling him with your fists and *kneeing* him?'

'I didn't knee him.'

'Lawson claims that you did.'

'I suppose, when it's put like that, it sounds bad.'

'You bet it does. It looks particularly bad when it's printed in black and white in an official letter of complaint. Jen, what in heaven's name were you thinking? We're a public relations firm. Your job is to control damage, not create it.'

'I'm sorry,' Jen said, trying to sound contrite, but missing the mark. Crikey, there was a good chance that if Harry Ryder walked into her office right now she'd consider creating a lot more damage—like a rearrangement of his smug facial features, especially his luscious lips.

Last night, when she'd watched him kissing Lisa, he'd managed to ruin the final few shreds of her fragile self-esteem. *And now he'd caused her to lose her job?* 'I can't believe I'm being fired because of one man. I mean one incident.'

'Well, if you must know, we'd already heard along the grapevine about a disruption involving you at Maurice Mannix's launch last week. I hadn't been going to mention it, but now…'

Jen groaned. That disruption had been Harry's fault too.

'We're within our rights to terminate your employment,' Sandi added. 'You're still on probation with us and these incidents suggest you're unsuitable.'

'Oh, good grief.' Jen pressed a hand to her throbbing temples and felt the proverbial grey cloud descending over her, fogging her vision, filling her nostrils, gagging her mouth. This was what it felt like to be a complete and utter failure. Last night had been bad enough; she'd never dreamed that her life could get any worse. 'Isn't there anything I can do?'

'There's one thing that might save you.'

'What is it? I'll do anything.'

'Eat dirt.'

'I beg your pardon?'

'Track down H R Taggart and grovel.'

But I don't want to set eyes on that jerk in this lifetime.

'I'm talking *serious grovelling*, Jen. Apologise to the poor man.'

'But he—'

'Plead with him to speak to his publishers. It's the only chance we have of securing their account with us. We need Taggart to put in a good word. They'll listen to him. He's your only hope.'

No. No. No.

'If he can convince Eagle and Browne that he wasn't offended by your behaviour, you have a chance. It's in his hands—and yours.'

Oh, sure. The fact that she'd been totally offended by *Harry's* behaviour clearly didn't count for anything in this unjust world.

'Jen, are you there? I thought you said you were pals with the guy.'

'Not pals exactly—'

'If it was a simple misunderstanding, as you claim, it shouldn't be too hard to apologise.'

But grovelling? Pleading with Harry?

The gods of irony must be laughing at her—last night she'd vowed never to see

Harry again and now her brilliant career depended on her doing exactly that.

'Swallow your pride. Just use a little
friendly persuasion. Remember, your job's on
the line.'

'I suppose—I'll have to try.'

'Of course you will. Use some feminine
charm. Women have been doing it since Eve
flashed that apple under Adam's nose.'

'I'm afraid Jen's line is still busy,' the receptionist told Harry. 'Can I take a message?'

'No, thank you,' he said. 'Just tell her I
called and I'll try to be in touch later.'

As he depressed the button on his phone he
felt confused, surprised by the strength of his
disappointment. It kicked low and hard, catching him off guard.

His impatience to be with Jen was unexpected, but since he'd left her place the night
before last memories of her had stayed with
him, disturbing his sleep and teasing their way
into his daytime thoughts.

This morning he'd risen early to write a scene for his current novel and not a single word had hit his computer screen. He'd sat at the keyboard, planning to write about murder and mayhem and felt a crazy urge to write a love scene instead. Problem was, his hero didn't have time to make love. The guy had villains to catch, the world to save.

Eventually he'd abandoned his work, wandered into the kitchen to make coffee, and then he'd gone outside on to the back porch and watched the sun rise over suburban rooftops, hoping for inspiration.

But, as the clouds grew pink, he'd thought of Jen's flushed cheeks and he cursed himself that he'd walked away from the secret warm pleasure of kissing her. He'd always considered himself to be a rather straightforward bloke, but these days he couldn't understand his own behaviour.

How had he got himself to this point? He'd been right to walk away, so why couldn't he get this woman out of his head? He knew that if he was the last man on earth he would be wrong for her. She needed Mr Nice Guy. But all he could think of now was how badly he wanted her. And it would have to be soon. Very soon.

Before she could recover from Sandi's bombshell Jen received another phone call—from Lisa this time.

'I wanted to thank you for all your help before I take off again,' her sister said.

Unable to hide her surprise, Jen let out a choked cry of disbelief. 'You're going away again? Already?'

'I'm heading up to the Sunshine Coast. I need a break. A getaway. And I want Millicent with me.'

'That will be great. It's a good idea,' Jen agreed, forcing warmth into her voice. She felt like she needed a break, too—a chance to escape from her life! 'I was surprised you had the energy to go out last night, Lisa,' she couldn't help adding.

'Oh? You know about that? Well, yes. It was a—a spur of the moment thing. As soon as I saw that chauffeur Mum sent—the one you lined up for Millicent—I knew he would be perfect. Just what I needed.'

'How fortunate,' Jen said, amazed that she kept her voice beneath a roar. 'And—and dare I ask what you—um—needed him for?'

'Not yet. It's too soon. I don't want to jinx my chances.' Lisa sounded nervous and Jen couldn't help wondering if her sister had fallen for Harry at first sight. Sickening green waves of jealousy curdled the morning coffee which lay percolating in her stomach. 'Are you taking Harry with you?'

Lisa laughed. 'No. It's only a couple of hours' drive to the beach. I don't need a chauffeur.'

Jen felt ridiculously light-headed with relief.

'I need to finish packing, Jen, so I can't stay and talk, but thanks again for looking after my little duck so beautifully.'

'That's OK,' Jen said faintly. 'She's a darling. I loved having her.'

As Jen replaced the receiver it occurred to her that caring for Millicent had been a breeze compared with her latest dilemma. Crumbs, how on earth was she going to persuade Harry Ryder to help her save her career?

Simply having to speak to him would be bad enough, but grovelling...pleading? No way. Why should she when it was his fault she'd landed in this mess? And why would he want to go out of his way to put a case to his publishers on her behalf? She was the Plain Jane he kept rushing away from.

If she was going to get him to do this she would have to pack some extra firing power. Her only chance of success was to plan her approach as carefully as she planned a PR campaign. She would have to target Harry the way she targeted a specialised market. Her presentation would be vitally important. And her image.

Her image was dormouse. Oh, heck. Finally, after years of her mother's warnings, she was going to have to do something about her grooming and wardrobe.

*   *   *

'I'm going shopping, Cleo,' she told the surprised receptionist.

'Shopping?' the girl repeated, her eyebrows arcs of mild accusation as she glanced pointedly at the clock.

Jen smiled sweetly. 'Something important's come up and I have to give it priority. Will you take my calls?'

'Of course. Actually, there have been a couple of calls already this morning, but your line was busy.'

'Anyone important?'

Cleo handed her a page torn from the message pad. 'They were both from Harry Ryder.'

A small grenade seemed to burst in Jen's chest and she struggled to breathe. She couldn't possibly deal with Harry yet. She wasn't ready. But the last thing she wanted was for Cleo to guess how crazily her private and professional lives had become enmeshed.

'Oh, just Harry?' she said and she was proud of the way she managed to give a careless little shrug. 'He's not important.'

To prove her point she screwed the piece of paper into a tiny ball, tossed it into the waste paper bin and continued towards the door.

She had a personal campaign to launch. She wasn't looking forward to any of it, but wasn't the longest journey supposed to start with a single step?

In the doorway she turned back, her gaze resting thoughtfully on Cleo. The girl was about twenty, a slim and pretty blonde. Trendy looking.

'Do you go to nightclubs, Cleo?'

'Um...' Cleo's mouth pulled into a self-conscious, puzzled smile. 'Yes, I do. Why?'

'I was wondering if you could recommend a good place to shop for something eye-catching.'

'To wear to a nightclub?'

'That style of thing.'

'Are you looking for classy or vamp?'

'Oh, ah—' Jen gulped. 'Vamp, I guess.'

'Eye-catching...vamp,' Cleo repeated and Jen wished she didn't look quite so amused.

'I'd say you should try Marco Jones in Albert Street.'

'OK. Thanks.'

As Jen hurried outside the phone rang again and she heard Cleo say, 'Oh, Mr Ryder, she's *just* left. Would you like me to try to catch her?'

Jen fled.

'You mean she's been out shopping for three hours?' Harry asked when he rang mid-afternoon. It didn't sound at all like the conscientious Jen he knew.

'She probably went straight from the city on to another job,' the receptionist said, sounding a trifle embarrassed, as if she'd been disloyal to Jen by mentioning the shopping.

'You definitely told her that I rang earlier?'

'Yes—sir.'

'And you passed on the phone number of the house I'm staying at? I don't think she had that before.'

'I—er—yes.'

'You don't sound too sure.'

'I'm sure I handed it to her,' the girl said, but an edginess in her voice gave Harry cold comfort.

'I'd really like to speak to her this afternoon. I hope you'll impress that on her.'

'I will, definitely.'

It was four p.m. by the time Jen got back to the office. 'I suppose there are one or two messages?' she said to Cleo.

'One or two.' Cleo handed her a sheet crowded with a list of messages, names and phone numbers and Jen scanned the list, relieved to see that Harry's name wasn't there.

'I left Mr Ryder's name off the list,' Cleo said.

Jen's head snapped up and she felt her cheeks flush. 'He rang again?'

'Several times.' Cleo was watching her reaction with obvious interest. 'But you told me he wasn't important. I got the impression—'

'You're right,' Jen said hastily. 'Harry Ryder's not at all important.' She shot a quick glance at the waste basket where she'd thrown his address and phone number this morning and then again at the list of names on the sheet she held. 'This is great. Thanks, Cleo.'

In her office she sat with her hands pressed to her heated cheeks and took slow breaths in and out through her nose, then dialled the limo agency's number.

'Could you put me through to Harry Ryder, please?' she asked the woman at the central office.

'Is that Miss Summers?'

'Yes.' Jen wasn't surprised that her voice had been recognised. She'd spoken to the woman on several occasions over the past week.

'Oh, Miss Summers, Harry's finished working for us. The man he was replacing started back on the job again today.'

'I see. Do you—do you have another contact? A home number, perhaps?'

'I'm sorry.' The woman made a sympathetic clucking sound. 'It's against company policy to provide that information. We have to protect our employees' privacy.'

'Yes, of course. I wasn't thinking. Thanks, anyway.' Collapsing forward with a groan, she propped her elbows on the desk, supporting her head in her hands. If only she hadn't been so cavalier with the note Cleo handed her this morning. If she couldn't find Harry the expensive shopping and hours stolen from the office would be wasted.

Lisa had already left for her undisclosed address at the Sunshine Coast, so she couldn't even swallow her pride and ask her sister if she had Harry's home number. But she had to find him; the next stage of her plan to save her job depended on it.

Her options were limited.

She could lose face with Cleo and admit she needed Harry's number—or she could raid the wastepaper basket. She'd lost enough face in recent times. The options narrowed to one.

As soon as Cleo headed for the bathroom Jen charged into the outer office and, with the speed of an action hero dodging bullets, shot across the carpet and dived under the desk. She had to sort through a mess of sticky sweet wrappers until she found half a dozen screwed up pieces of memo paper in the basket. And then she had to unfold every single one before she found the scrap with Harry's contact details including a street address in Coorparoo.

'Jen, are you OK?'

Cleo's voice sounded close behind her. Jen jumped and banged her head on the desk.

Struggling to her feet, she sent Cleo a glare sufficiently glacial to ensure her silence and, with her head haughtily high, she refrained from explaining what she was doing and sailed back into her own office without making further eye contact.

Two hours later Jen spritzed a cloud of perfume over her bare shoulders and arms and outlined her lips with a vibrant lipstick called Sunset Jungle.

Tonight a very different reflection looked back from her bedroom mirror. Her sedate navy blue silk dress had given way to a flirty, fiery red affair. The dress's shoestring straps and scarily low, scooped neckline made it look more like a petticoat than a proper dress.

Chains of glittering gold coins dangled from her earlobes. Her shoes comprised little more than ultra expensive strips of gold leather with very high heels. She looked like a vamp and felt like a tramp.

'I've gone too far,' she said out loud. 'The neckline is too low.' She pulled at the top of the dress in a desperate endeavour to cover her cleavage. 'The skirt's too short.' Tugging at the hemline made the cleavage reappear. 'The red's wrong.'

Red wasn't her colour. It had never been her colour. She was a brown girl. She preferred beige. She *loved* beige.

'Everything about this look is too—too *not* me.'

But then again—a small inner voice whispered—that was the point of this exercise.

The girl in the shop had been sure this dress was what she needed.

'What are you looking for?' she'd asked.

'I need the dress most likely to make a man who doesn't seem interested in me do something for me that he doesn't particularly want to do,' Jen had explained.

To her credit, the girl had only looked boggle-eyed for a moment before she headed straight for this dress.

'You can't miss with this,' she'd said emphatically.

But Jen was only now fully aware of the enormous gap between an idea and its execution. She had the kind of dress that was supposed to impress men like Harry, but how could she manufacture the right attitude?

And was it possible to transform one's personality in the mere twenty minutes it took to drive across the city to Harry's place? After what she'd witnessed at the theatre last night could she find the courage to charm him?

With a rush of panic she remembered that she had no choice. Her job was at stake. She couldn't afford to let Harry escape until she got what she wanted.

CHAPTER EIGHT

IT WAS still early in the evening and not quite dark as Polly set the dining table for herself and Harry. Through the long sash windows, opened wide to catch the breeze, Harry contemplated the view of his grandmother's back garden. Earlier in the afternoon he'd mowed the lawn and now the earthy, sweet smell of freshly cut grass drifted towards him.

Petals loosened from the heavy heads of summer roses floated over the lawn, making fat splashes of white that turned pearlescent in the wash of lavender twilight.

The evening star, winking in an aquamarine sky, made a stunning backdrop for the purple-flowering jacaranda tree guarding the back of the house. From the shrubbery by the back fence came the peep-peep-peeping of crickets and he felt a rush of nostalgia for his childhood.

Holidays at Gran's. In this very garden he and his brothers had spent bright mornings hunting for lizards in the rockery, long summer afternoons eating watermelon and having hose fights, warm nights playing hide and seek.

He'd always felt so much more at one with his family when he'd been here.

He waved a hand to take in his grandmother's pretty dining room and the view through the window. 'I've enjoyed staying with you so much,' he told her.

Delight flashed in her eyes. 'I'm going to miss you.'

'I'll miss you, too, sweetheart. *And* this,' he added, indicating the meal she'd prepared—lamb cutlets, creamy mashed potatoes, bundles of steamed baby carrots and minted peas.

They took their seats and Polly smiled as she smoothed a starched napkin on her lap. 'You've enjoyed your stint as a chauffeur, haven't you?'

'Most of it.'

'Particularly running around with little Millicent. That was an interesting experience for you.'

Harry's eyebrows lifted. 'I guess interesting is an appropriate word to describe it.'

They began to eat but, after a minute or two, Polly stopped cutting her food and looked at him. 'I'm so sorry I didn't get to meet Millicent's Jen.'

He frowned and wished he didn't feel a hollow kind of emptiness when Jen's name was mentioned. Why hadn't she returned his calls? 'I think you would have got on well with her,' he said.

'I know.'

'You *know*?' He swallowed quickly. 'How can you be so sure of her if you didn't meet her?'

Polly laughed lightly. 'Because she sounds sensible.'

'Oh, she's sensible all right. She's domesticated, competent, the kind of girl people turn to in a crisis.'

'The kind of girl you've always gone out of your way to avoid.'

'Too true,' he growled. Time to drop this subject. His grandmother could be a terrier when she found a topic she wanted to analyse, hanging on and worrying it like a bone until she unearthed exactly what she wanted to know. 'Jen's not my type at all,' he said.

'And yet,' Polly said, 'she had such a positive impact on you.'

'What are you talking about?'

Setting her knife and fork carefully on her plate, she reached out a wrinkled hand to pat his arm. 'I've known you all your life, my boy, and I might be old but I can see a change. Take the other night, for example. Instead of painting the town red with one of your dolly birds, you felt compelled to drive over to Jen's place with Millicent's violin, even though a simple phone call would have set their minds at rest.'

'The kid needed to practise.'

'You didn't know that when you set out. Then, on Saturday night, you stayed home and worked on your book. No dolly birds then, either.'

'I have a deadline.'

'That didn't bother you on any other Saturday night.'

Harry refused to comment. He speared a carrot with his fork and stared at it.

'Then you attended Millicent's recital on Sunday.'

'OK,' he admitted, grudgingly. 'I've developed a soft spot for Millicent. She's kinda cute and she's very talented. She intrigues me. I like people with talent.'

'And was it Millicent's talent that sent you hightailing off to Jen's on Monday night with a bottle of wine?'

Leaning back in his chair, Harry stared at his grandmother. 'Now you're just getting carried away.'

'I wish *you* would, Harry.'

'What do you mean?'

'I wish you could be totally carried away and fall in love.'

'I've been in love thousands of times.'

'Humph.' Polly sighed and picked up her knife and fork again. 'If the good Lord answers my prayers, some day soon you'll fall completely head over heels and you won't know what's hit you.'

Harry smiled and then, just to tease her, he shuddered. After a beat, he added, 'Why don't you ask me if it was an interest in Jen Summers that sent me to the theatre last night with her glamorous sister?'

'So the sister's glamorous, is she? What about Jen?'

Harry pulled his brow into an exaggerated frown as if he hadn't given the matter much thought. 'She's different. She doesn't stand out like her sister and she likes to make herself disappear by wearing camouflage colours.'

'You mean she doesn't try to draw attention to herself.'

'That's right. She—'

A knock at the door interrupted Polly. 'I wonder who that could be?'

'I'll get it.' Harry pushed his chair back.

'No dear, you stay there.' Polly could be surprisingly nimble and now she sprang to her feet. 'It's probably my neighbour. She has a young baby and can't always get to the shops and she's frequently running out of something.'

Jen was scared. Witless. Here she was at Harry's front door and she'd already forgotten her carefully composed greeting.

Right now all she could think was that she mustn't mention last night at the theatre. If she started on that topic she might lose her cool and tonight she needed to be mega-cool and focused. She'd had twenty minutes to reinvent herself and now she was supposed to be an uninhibited and carefree creature, thinking of nothing but flirtation and her goal—a secure if not brilliant career.

Footsteps approached from within the house and she forced herself to breathe deeply. Problem was, deep breaths in a low-cut dress left a girl in danger of a boob-falling-out emergency.

The door opened.

A tiny old lady with soft white hair, sweet apple cheeks and gentle brown eyes peeped out at her. Jen slammed her clutch purse over her exposed bosom.

'Hello,' the old lady said, smiling.

'Oh, I'm sorry. I think I must have the wrong address.'

'Perhaps you're looking for my grandson?'

'Your grandson?' An instant picture of a skinny boy of six or seven complete with a missing front tooth and a scraped knee floated before her. 'No, I'm sorry to have disturbed you.'

'His name is Harry. Harry Ryder.'

'Oh!' Jen's face burst into flames. Harry was living with his grandmother? This was so embarrassing. What a disaster. She knew she should have phoned first, but she'd opted to use surprise as a line of attack. Now it had backfired bang in her face.

There was no way she'd go into Harry's grandmother's house in this too tiny dress, with this heavy make-up and come-to-bed sultry perfume. She had to get away. 'I—er—I'd better go.'

'Is it someone for me?' came a deep, familiar voice from within the house.

Jen's heart leapt to her throat as she shook her head at the woman and turned, scurrying back down the steep wooden stairs as fast as her spindly high heels would allow. She needed the safety of the gathering darkness. This was *so* wrong!

'It's a young lady,' she heard the old woman say, 'but she says she doesn't know you, Harry.'

A light flashed on and a yellow glow spilled down the stairs, exposing Jen like a rabbit caught in the glare of a car's headlights.

'Jen, is that you?'

Oh, God. She looked back over her shoulder and saw Harry's silhouette towering beside his grandmother's in the open doorway. A gusty breeze whipped at her short skirt, lifting it high to display her bare thighs, and she batted at the skirt, making ineffectual attempts to hold it down, but her frantic efforts caused one of her spaghetti thin straps to slip from her shoulder. *Oh, good grief!*

To her right a shadow moved and a sleek black cat slipped silently into the leafy haven of shrubbery beside the stairs. She would give anything, *anything*, to be able to disappear like that.

'Jen,' Harry called. 'Don't run away. Come on inside.'

'Is this Jen?' his grandmother cried. 'My goodness, dear, why didn't you tell me you were Millicent's Jen? Please, come in. Have you eaten?'

Jen gulped as she dragged her strap back into place. What could she do? How could she explain her attire? Harry's sweet little grandmother would be shocked if she knew she'd dressed like a vamp in the expectation of finding her grandson alone.

'I don't want to interrupt your meal,' she said from halfway down the stairs.

'Don't worry,' the grandmother said. 'I always cook a little extra. Do come in and join us.' Her smile was beatific as she held out her hands to Jen and she didn't seem at all per-turbed by the skimpy dress. 'I'm Polly McLean.'

'Lovely to meet you.' With a sinking heart, Jen came back to the top of the steps and shook the proffered hand. 'But truly, don't go to the bother of feeding me. I—I was only popping in for a moment.'

Her gaze slid cautiously to Harry. Unlike his grandmother, he made no attempt to mask his puzzled amusement and he seemed very interested in the particulars of her attire.

'I'll leave you to talk to Harry.' Polly beamed at them as if they were both very good children who'd pleased her greatly. 'Take your time, dears. I'll pop back to the kitchen and keep our meals warm in the oven.'

She bustled away, leaving a red-faced Jen alone with Harry in the small front room.

Harry adopted a casual pose with a hand propped high against the doorjamb and his smile did little to put her at ease. 'You're all dressed up,' he said. 'Are you going some-where?'

'Yes,' she lied hastily. What was the point of telling the truth now? 'I'm—um—I'm on my way into town for a girls' night out.'

'Off to a nightclub?'

'A nightclub? Yes, that's it.'

'Which one?'

'Ah—' *Help!* Jen's mind raced. She'd been living in Sydney for so long she was no longer familiar with any of Brisbane's trendy night-clubs. 'I forget which one the girls decided on. I'm meeting them first in—in the city.'

His hand came away from the wall as he straightened slowly, crossing his arms over his chest and squaring his shoulders, seeming to grow taller, broader and more intimidating as he cast another amused glance over her dress. 'Looks like you're ready for fun.'

'Of course. We always have loads of fun.'

He nodded slowly, his eyes more thought-ful, although the smile lingered and played at the corners of his mouth. 'And so you called in at my grandmother's house on your way to a nightclub. How interesting, Jen. I can only assume you also wanted to see me about something?'

With an overwhelming sense of dread, Jen realised that this was it. The moment to launch her request. But she'd reached it too soon or by the wrong route; it felt so wrong.

It made no sense at all to be standing in this tiny dress in the front room at his grand-mother's house. Instead of feeling alluring she felt awkward, exposed and powerless.

'I need your help,' she said, diving in with the unthinking, panicky dread of someone who has no choice but to bathe in icy water. 'I'm in danger of losing my job.'

Her intense embarrassment pushed her to add, childishly, 'And it's your fault.'

'I've lost you your job?' Harry said and one of his eyebrows hiked to show how incredible he found her accusation.

But, to her relief, he listened patiently while she told him about the complaint from Lawson's Bookstore. 'I need you to speak up for me with your publishers or I might lose my position.'

He shrugged. 'Yeah, sure. I'll speak to them.'

Jen was gobsmacked. Her jaw dropped. 'Just like that?'

A little red dress works this quickly?

'It's no problem,' Harry said. 'I'll speak to them first thing tomorrow morning.'

'Thanks. That's great. Thank you.'

He flashed her a brief, wolfish smile. 'But first you must say please very nicely.'

And then, with the unexpected, silent speed of a jungle predator, he closed the gap between them and his hand caught hold of hers, pulling her close.

Surprise snatched her breath and sent warmth flushing through her. 'Please very nicely,' she repeated, trying for a coquettish smile but fearing she looked foolish.

His fingers played with her dress strap. It had fallen again, but when he hooked it back on to her shoulder his hand stayed there, tracing a slow, sensuous spiral on her skin.

Jen felt trapped in an electrified net. The red dress was working. She no longer looked like a dormouse. Harry was interested. But she'd already achieved her goal. What was she supposed to do now?

If she jumped away Harry might change his mind and refuse her request, but if she stayed who knew what he might do? And if his grandmother walked in she would feel such a tramp.

At least she was holding Harry's attention, which was a marked improvement on the other times she'd been alone with him. Her eyes watched in a haze of heated fascination as Harry's hand moved down, tracing the neckline of her dress over the swell of her breasts.

'So, are you definitely going to help me, Harry?'

'Of course,' he murmured as he continued to trail his fingertips over her skin. 'We agreed the other night that the problem would never have arisen if I'd been more honest with you.'

Honest? Jen almost backed away. Did Harry Ryder know the meaning of the word? What about last night with Lisa? When was he going to mention that?

A small, mocking chuckle sounded close to her ear. 'You're not a clubber, are you, Jen? You're not on your way to a girls' night out.'

'I—I.' How dared he accuse her of dishonesty? If only his touch wasn't wrecking her control she would think of a smart response.

He was enjoying his teasing cat-and-mouse game. Last night he'd been kissing her sister and tonight he was toying with her. She stood as stiffly as a sentry guard while his fingers travelled relentlessly on, making her senses scream.

She heard another soft chuckle. 'Jen, I can't believe you came here to offer yourself to me to save your job.'

Her heart bucked in a shocked, shamed leap. 'I came to reason with you,' she protested and, in spite of her dismay, she forced her chin haughtily high. 'I had no plans to sleep with you!'

'No?' His eyes burned her.

'Absolutely not. We agreed the other night that it wasn't an option.'

'I've been rethinking that decision.' Once more his lazy smile travelled over her and the heated challenge in his eyes stole her breath. Lifting his hand to her face, his thumb trailed across the seam of her lips, teasing them apart. She was too surprised, too mesmerised, to do anything but submit to his exploration. His broad thumb touched her teeth, the tip of her tongue. She could taste him.

'You want me,' he murmured.

Oh, mercy. Even if she'd known how to answer him she couldn't have made her voice work.

A light step sounded in the hallway and Harry's grandmother called, 'Jen, you will change your mind and have a bite to eat with us, won't you? I've dished up an extra serving.'

She tried to speak, tried to refuse, but Harry covered her mouth with his hand and called, 'Yes, thanks, Polly. Jen's joining us.'

'But—' Jen's eyes implored him to set her free. He dropped his hand to his side. 'This dress—'

'Is fantastic,' he said, grinning. 'Come on. You're all dressed up with nowhere to go and my grandmother does a great lamb cutlet. Besides, Polly is a big fan of yours.'

A fan? She doesn't know me. How can she be a fan? Jen stared at him, puzzled.

But he didn't reply, simply took her by the elbow and nudged her towards the hallway. 'Come.'

Polly was waiting just outside the dining room. 'I've kept everything warm,' she said, cheeks dimpling and eyes sparkling.

'Thanks,' Harry said.

He led Jen to a newly set place at the dining table and watched the appreciation in her eyes as she took in the scene—Polly's pretty blue vase of Iceberg roses set in the table's centre, the sparkling silver and immaculate white tablecloth with blue embroidery around its scalloped edge—the shadowy, starlit garden beyond.

And, as he performed the small courtesy of helping her with her chair, he watched the bloom of pink in her cheeks and did his manful best not to let his gaze drift elsewhere…to the sweet symmetry of her neck and shoulders…the lush curves of her perfect breasts…the peachy softness of her skin.

The scarlet, hardly-there dress was so different from Jen's usual dress code. It was going to be slow torture to sit across the table from her, trying not to look and not to think about touching her.

How on earth had he ever walked away from this woman? He must have had rocks in his head.

Polly returned with their meals and Jen murmured her appreciation, but for the most part they ate in silence, conscious that the meal had already been interrupted and delayed.

Then Polly said, 'Are you going to the theatre this evening, Jen?'

Her head snapped up quickly and her deep brown eyes took on such a guarded wariness that Harry realised for the first time that Lisa Summers might not have explained to her sister about her plan for the previous evening. 'No, not the theatre,' she said, shaking her head vigorously.

'I thought you might have been going to the symphony concert,' Polly persisted.

'There was only one performance and that was last night,' Harry cut in, hoping his grandmother heeded the warning note in his frown and voice.

Polly didn't. 'Harry went to the theatre last night,' she said, shooting a smile of calculated innocence his way.

The air in the dining room seemed to chill by several degrees. Jen's chin lifted and Harry saw a flash of steely vehemence in her eyes. 'I know Harry was there,' she said.

'So Lisa filled you in on her plans?' he asked hopefully.

'No,' she said coldly, quietly. 'She was very mysterious about last night, but *I* was there. I saw you.'

Harry frowned at her. 'Why on earth didn't you speak to us?'

Her gaze dropped to her plate and she poked at some peas with her fork. 'I—I didn't stay for very long.'

He saw the tightness of her mouth as she sat, stabbing peas with her eyes downcast, and couldn't help imagining that same mouth softening, warming and coming alive beneath his, such a very different experience from when the photographers had urged him to kiss Lisa.

He felt an unfamiliar pang of guilt. Polly was watching him, accusation fierce in her eyes, and he knew what his grandmother was thinking—that he'd hurt Millicent's Jen, just as she'd feared he would.

And no doubt it was true. Hell, two nights ago he'd walked away from the willing warmth of Jen's arms and the following evening he'd made a spectacle of himself, kissing her sister in public.

How did he explain that now? How could he expect her to understand that for Harry Ryder it was far safer to share harmless kisses in public with a woman he didn't particularly care for than to spend a night in private with one he might like too much.

He leaned towards Jen, anxious to make amends. 'Didn't your sister mention that she'd asked me to help her out?'

She pressed a hand against her chest and her worried eyes sought his. 'Help her out? What do you mean?'

'Practically the first thing Lisa did when I drove Millicent to her place was to beg me to accompany her to the concert. She'd just found out about it and she wanted someone to accompany her—any man who was tall and reasonably presentable.' He shrugged and heard a faint *'humph'* come from Polly's end of the table.

Jen shook her head. 'It doesn't make sense. Why did she have to race off to a concert when she'd just got back from Perth?'

'Because of Michael Wolfe, of course.'

'O-o-o-h.' Understanding and curiosity flared in her eyes.

'I told her about Wolfe's interest in Millicent at the recital and she practically pounced on me and asked me a hundred questions.'

'Really?' Jen was highly interested now.

'Did you know that Michael Wolfe is Millicent's father?'

'Lisa told you that?'

'Yes.'

'Oh, my God. Mum and I could never get her to admit it,' she said, her voice rising with excitement. 'But I *knew* it. I thought he was the one.'

'Your sister's desperate to get back together with him. So desperate she wanted to make him jealous and was prepared to—' He paused and remembered Polly was sitting at the table with them, watching and listening.

'I saw exactly what she was prepared to do,' Jen said darkly.

Their eyes met and Harry was hit by a slam of regret. 'My only reason for agreeing to go was because I feel quite strongly that Millicent needs a father,' he said.

'Yes,' Jen agreed. 'She certainly does.' Their gazes held for the longest time. Harry smiled and willed her to understand that kissing Lisa had meant nothing. Nothing.

Perhaps the message reached her because, after some moments, her face was transformed by an answering smile that started tentatively at first but grew gradually warmer like a beautiful sunrise. 'So, was my sister successful in her quest?'

'I don't expect to hear the final outcome. My job was merely to accompany her for the evening, stick close to her in the Green Room after the show and pay her plenty of attention. But, if the black looks on Wolfe's face were anything to go by, I'd say a measure of success was achieved. The rest is up to them.'

He shrugged. 'Actually, I rather liked what I saw of the guy. Under other circumstances, I would have liked to get to know him better.'

'Well, Lisa and Millicent have gone away to the Sunshine Coast today. I hope Michael Wolfe's gone with them.'

Harry gave a brief shrug. He was fast losing interest in the fate of Lisa and Michael. It seemed suddenly irrelevant as he sat there staring at Jen, trying to read her mood.

'Jen...' he said, then stopped when he remembered that Polly was sitting at the table with them.

'So,' Jen said. 'Now that you've finished your stint as a chauffeur will you be taking off again? I imagine that you could write a novel from anywhere if you had a word processor.'

Harry winced, caught up sharply by her sudden question and wishing he had a different answer. 'Yes,' he admitted. 'I'm already booked to fly to Hong Kong in a couple of days' time.'

Polly made a noise that sounded suspiciously like a disgusted snort and Jen gave an awkward little smile, then deftly switched the conversation by asking a question about his grandmother's house and garden.

After that, the conversation steered into safe, suburban waters as Polly and Jen chatted about flower end rot in tomatoes, but Harry was seized by a restless urgency to discuss more personal matters. In private.

As soon as they finished eating he glanced at his wrist-watch and turned to his grandmother. 'You're missing the start of your favourite television show. Let me bring you a cup of coffee in the living room and leave me to do the dishes.'

'Don't be ridiculous, boy,' Polly snapped.

'Since when has common courtesy become ridiculous?'

'Never, but you're overlooking a more important courtesy.' Polly sent a quick sideways smile towards Jen. 'You should be escorting this young lady home—or—or wherever she wishes to go.'

Harry stared at his grandmother, momentarily stunned by her blatant manipulation. He was quite capable of making his own moves.

'There's no need,' Jen cut in quickly. 'I have my car.'

'No, let me drive you,' Harry said, his pulse racing at this golden opportunity to hurry back to Jen's place, to be alone with her. He offered her a smooth grin. 'I've had a great deal of recent experience on the roads and I've excellent driving credentials.'

Jen wet her lips as if they were suddenly dry and Harry's insides tied themselves into a dozen knots as he watched her consider his offer for several long moments. Then she gave a sorry little shake of her head. 'Thanks, Harry, but I can't impose on you. You've already done enough for me by offering to speak to Eagle and Browne in the morning. And you've done so much for my family— driving Millicent, helping Lisa. You've been magnificent.'

She turned towards Polly and the pretty gold coins dangling from her ears swung and gleamed, catching the light. 'Thank you so much for dinner, Mrs McLean; it was delicious.'

She was leaving. Harry drew in a sharp breath as surprise mingled with acute disappointment. He'd been sure he'd read her correctly—the provocative dress, the promise in her smile…

As Jen stood and his grandmother rose too, he jumped to his feet and was surprised anew by the way Polly held out her hands to Jen and sent her a pleased, knowing wink.

What was going on here? One minute the old girl was trying to push them together, now she seemed pleased as Punch that her plan had failed. Women! They got more difficult to fathom as they got older!

He felt unexpectedly adrift, like a vessel with its moorings cut. In the doorway, Jen paused and looked back at him and her eyes glittered with a sudden unnerving sheen. 'Goodbye, Harry,' she said.

His throat felt full of sharp gravel and he swallowed painfully. 'I'll phone you in the morning after I've spoken to my publishers.'

'Thanks.' She drew in a quick breath. 'Thank you for everything and—and good luck with your next book.' Then her lower lip began to tremble and she turned quickly and hurried out of the house.

Out of his life.

He'd never felt so suddenly empty, as if he'd been physically drained of something vital, like his blood.

'What are you grinning about?' he bellowed at Polly as he followed her through to the kitchen, carrying the dirty dishes.

The old lady's smile was secretive, enigmatic. 'I always knew that I'd like Millicent's Jen. She's the best thing that's happened to you in a long, long time, my dear boy.'

'You're dreaming, Polly.' Harry let out an angry growl as he dumped plates on the kitchen counter.

'Be careful. Don't break my best dinnerware.' Polly stepped closer and her gnarled hand rested lightly on his wrist. 'I love you, Harry, but if you're feeling bad right now I couldn't be happier.'

He glared at her, his breath coming in painful bursts. And she glared back. For long, conspicuous seconds he stood staring down at his fragile, birdlike, indomitable grandmother, and then finally he said, 'Leave the dishes. I'll do them in the morning.'

The grim expression in her eyes softened. 'So you're going—out?'

'Yeah.' He turned and headed for the door. 'Don't wait up.'

'By the way,' Polly called after him. 'I was very impressed by Jen's camouflage.'

After Jen parked her car she closed the garage door and leaned against it, balancing first on one leg and then the other as she slipped her aching feet out of her high-heeled shoes. Then she padded across the front lawn in her bare feet, feeling the grass, soft and springy between her toes, and the night air, fragrant with the scents of summer flowers, cool against her skin. Tonight had been a success. She should be celebrating.

Hey, she'd achieved her goal. Harry Ryder was going to talk to his publishers and, with luck, her job would remain secure. And, as an added bonus, he'd explained about his trip to the theatre with Lisa. All in all, the night had been nothing but good news right down to the possibility of a reconciliation for Lisa and Michael Wolfe—*and* a father for Millicent.

So why wasn't she skipping across the lawn? Why wasn't she deliriously happy? In fact, why did she feel a thousand times worse than she had last night when she'd come home from the theatre?

She released a sigh so deep it seemed to come from the earth beneath her toes and, as she sank on to the bottom of her front steps, it became a groan of despair. She let her head droop sideways against the timber balustrade and stared out into the dark, silent garden.

Was there ever a time when she'd felt so miserable? This evening had been the worst ordeal of her life. The very worst thing had happened. She'd joined Harry and his grandmother for dinner and watched the way Polly idolised him and her poor heart had taken a headlong dive.

She'd fallen completely in love.

Just like that.

Stupid. Stupid. Stupid. She'd plunged head over heels. Who would have thought she could fall in love with a man at the dinner table?

But here she was helplessly, hopelessly, foolishly in love.

Of course, if she were honest, she might admit that she'd been falling in love with Harry Ryder from the minute he'd marched into Maurice's salon but, however it had happened, tonight her heart had been captured.

By an impossible dream.

Impossible because Harry could never return her feelings. She just wasn't his type. Harry was too dangerous. Oh, he could be charming and sweet with Millicent and with his grandmother, but what about the rest of the time?

What about the Harry Ryder who had a bad-boy reputation in his outback home town? The devil-may-care H R Taggart, author of bloodcurdling novels? The restless wanderer, who'd walked away from her because he didn't want complications in his love life? *The jerk who'd been eager to seduce her tonight even though he was dashing off to Hong Kong in a day or two and might never see her again?*

Thank heavens she hadn't succumbed to his temptation. A parting fling with Harry would have left her even more desolate. She'd had no choice but to reject his offer to accompany her home. Now, alone and miserable, she huddled on her front steps, wrapped in her own lonely arms instead of his.

But there was no point in moping over such a lost cause like a silly teenager. Heavens, she was almost thirty—mature enough to accept that there was nothing to be gained by yearning for the wrong kind of man.

Gripping the stair rail, she dragged herself to her feet, but a distant sound made her pause and her heart drummed. From a few streets away came the throb of a motorbike's engine. Oh, mercy, it was coming closer. Was it Harry? It couldn't be.

Her nerves strained to snapping point as the bike roared down her street and shuddered to a halt in front of her house. In the glow of an overhead streetlight she watched a tall, black-clad figure dismount.

'Is that you, Jen?' Harry's deep voice reached her across the shadowy lawn.

She tried to answer but her throat wouldn't work. She wanted to dash inside the house and slam the door but her feet were rooted to the ground. Why had he followed her home?

Swiping at her damp eyes and cheeks with the backs of her hands, she watched as he removed his helmet, clipped it to his bike then came towards her, unzipping his leather jacket and moving with unhurried, easy strides.

It wasn't until he'd almost reached her that she prised her tongue from the roof of her mouth and managed to speak. 'What—what are you doing here? What do you want?' Standing in her bare feet, she felt dwarfed by his height.

'I wasn't happy with the way we parted,' he said, coming close, too close. 'I didn't want to let you go like that.'

'Like what?'

He flashed her a smile so sexy it sent her bare toes curling over the edge of the step. 'Without a kiss.'

A wave of giddy disbelief swept through her. *Don't do this to me, Harry.*

'It would be such a pity to miss out on at least one kiss after you went to the trouble of dressing up like this.'

'You know I didn't wear this dress to score a kiss.'

'Oh, yeah, I forgot.' His smile tilted, becoming one-sided, mocking. 'You were merely flaunting yourself to save your job.'

She should never have worn this stupid dress. How crazy she'd been to signal seduction. Harry took a bold step closer. He'd never looked sexier than he did now with his face half in shadow and his leather jacket bulking out his shoulders, making them broader than ever.

She heard a soft sound low in his throat and, without further warning, he reached for her waist and drew her against him. He was solid, warm and very male. His mouth on hers was soft and hard at once, coaxing and demanding, tender and hot.

The very first touch of his mouth weakened her resistance. Every part of her wanted this. His lips on hers, seeking deeper intimacy, promising her bliss as surely as spring brings the promise of summer. But, heaven help her, she couldn't surrender. Had to pull away. 'No, Harry!'

Without releasing his hold on her, he lifted his mouth a mere inch. 'What's the matter?' His face was entirely in shadow now, but she could hear the impatient rasp in his voice and could sense the glittering intensity in his eyes.

'Please, don't play games with me,' she whispered.

'Games?' A merciless chuckle broke from his lips. 'Sweetheart, you're the one who's all dressed up in the follow-me-home dress.'

She shook her head, knowing that if she tried to speak she would sob.

'I'm burning for you, Jen. I want you so badly.' His hands at her waist tugged her hips closer. 'This badly.'

Oh, help—she had never felt so engulfed by need.

And this was her own silly fault. If she'd been sensible and honest with herself she would have admitted when she'd bought the red dress that this was how the night would end. But she'd dived in, not allowing herself to think of the danger, and now she was out of her depth.

With her hands firmly in the middle of his chest, she struggled to hold herself back from Harry and from the licking flames of desire that threatened to overpower her.

'I'm sorry,' she cried. 'I'm sorry about the dress. I didn't mean to give the wrong impression. It—it seemed like a good idea at the time.'

'It was a great idea,' he said, his dark chocolate voice rumbling close to her ear, threatening to liquefy every bone in her body. Two of his fingers slipped beneath her shoulder strap. 'And I have an even better idea about what we should be doing with this dress right now.'

'Oh, please, don't,' she moaned. 'You said you don't want this. You don't want complications.'

'Forget what I said.' His warm lips nuzzled the side of her neck and behind her ear.

'I can't forget it, Harry. You were right.'

'No, I wasn't,' he murmured, touching his tongue to her earlobe.

'No!' she cried, pulling away forcefully, so forcefully at last, that Harry let her go and she stumbled back against the stair railing.

'What's the matter, Jen?' He stood before her with his suddenly empty hands dangling loosely by his sides.

Her breath came in panting spurts and her voice was half-choked by tears. 'I'm protecting myself.'

'I can see that, but why? Why the change? The other night you wanted this.'

'And the other night you said you didn't want anything complicated.' She dragged in another breath. 'I'm afraid this is getting complicated.'

'Maybe not,' he said. 'Perhaps I misread you.'

She shook her head. 'You didn't. I'm—' The embarrassing truth was so hard to get out, but she knew it was the one thing that would get through to him. 'I'm halfway in love with you, Harry.'

She saw the way he stiffened when he heard her confession and her heart felt as if it was exploding into a hundred pieces.

'I know you don't want a complication like—like love. And—and I don't want to make saying goodbye any harder for myself.' Her hand fluttered to cover her trembling lips as she fought back a sob. 'I'm sorry to admit this, but if we made love I'd end up completely in love with you and then I'd be a mess because you have no plans to stay, have you? You're off to Hong Kong in a day or two.'

Harry stared at Jen for long, pulsing seconds and with a sick heart she saw the impact of her confession slam into him and sink home. His head dropped forward and he low-

ered his gaze to stare at the ground that sep-
arated them.

She watched as he drew in a deep breath
and let it out again on a long, slow sigh. The
night seemed to gather in close around them,
as if it was as desperate as she was to hear
his response.

'You're right,' he said after some time.
Dragging a hand across his grim mouth, he
shook his head slowly as his bleak gaze wandered sideways to take in the garden and her
house. He looked as if he'd been slugged.
'You need some nice, steady house-and-
garden, salt of the earth kind of guy.'

His chest rose and fell as he inhaled again
and exhaled slowly and he shoved his hands
deep into his pockets. He groaned. 'I'm damn
sorry, Jen. I rushed over here without thinking—I guess it was a case of my brains dropping below my belt. You look so damn sexy
tonight and—'

Jen gulped. She had never expected a man
like Harry would say she looked sexy. She

needed to cry, but she was determined not to sob all over him.

He stepped close to her again and touched her elbow with his fingertips, leaned forward and kissed her damp cheek. 'Take care, brown girl.'

Her scalding throat was too blocked by tears to answer. She nodded and kept her eyes lowered as he turned to walk slowly back along her front path to his bike. Then, unable to bear another farewell, she stumbled up her steps and shoved her key into the lock.

She didn't look back as she heard the gate swing shut and she was deep inside her house by the time she heard the bike's motor rev, then take off with a roar, racing away from her into the night. For the last time.

CHAPTER NINE

HARRY woke from restless dreams to a feeling of dread. Sweat-dampened sheets were tangled around his legs and his stomach roiled as he fought his way through a fog of semi-consciousness, struggling to fathom the source of his panicky nervousness.

Then he remembered Jen and the pain in her face when she'd admitted she was falling for him. Hell, he hadn't wanted to hurt her. What a jerk he'd been to tease her last night and then chase after her like a wild tom-cat. It had been so wrong to pursue her when he knew she was the kind of girl who gave her heart and soul when she shared her body.

When he knew he had no right to her heart or soul.

Kicking against the nightmarish tightness of the sheets that bound his legs, he prepared to fight an extended battle with his conscience but the telephone began to ring shrilly in the kitchen and he welcomed the distraction. Tumbling out of bed, he staggered down the hall in his boxer shorts to answer it.

Polly beat him to it. She was already up and neatly dressed in a blue cotton frock, with bacon frying on the stove and a pot of tea and two mugs set on the kitchen table. 'I'll just get Harry for you,' he heard her say into the phone. 'Your agent,' she whispered as she handed the receiver to him.

'Good morning, Reg.' Harry yawned and stretched.

'Morning, Harry. Listen, mate. I need your reassurance that you can answer the allegations in today's *Gazette*.'

Harry blinked and frowned as he ran his fingers through sleep-tousled hair. 'What allegations? What are you talking about?'

'You haven't seen the paper yet?'

'Give a man a break, Reg. It's the crack of dawn.' He'd spent far too much of last night wide awake, wrestling with tortured thoughts.

'Then you'd better take a look at it and ring me straight back,' Reg told him.

Harry winced and sighed. 'OK.' To Polly he grumbled, 'What time is it, anyway? Who's supposed to have read the paper at this hour?'

'It's only six-thirty. I haven't brought the paper in yet,' she said. 'Perhaps your agent's forgotten that Queensland's an hour behind New South Wales in summer.'

'Yeah,' he growled, and yawned and stretched again like a lazy lion. As he padded back through the house to his bedroom to collect a T-shirt he scratched thoughtfully at his chest. Reg's tone had been just a little too edgy for his liking. He shoved thoughts of Jen aside as he tried to make sense of his agent's cryptic instructions.

But he only felt mild curiosity as he headed for the front lawn to collect the paper. He had no premonition that his life was about to spin out of control.

An hour later, Jen, dressed ready for work, perched on a stool at her breakfast bar. She couldn't face anything more than a glass of freshly squeezed orange juice for breakfast and, needing a distraction from her frenzied thoughts about Harry, she aimed the remote control at the small television set in the corner of the room and tuned in to a breakfast news channel.

Oh, my God.

Harry filled her screen. Barefoot and dressed in his shorts and a T-shirt, he was standing in his grandmother's front garden, shaking a newspaper at a pack of journalists. As the pack crowded in on him, cameras whirring, he held the paper over his face to hide behind it.

'This was the scene in the front of a Coorparoo home this morning when our reporters tried to interview the well-known author, H R Taggart,' a newsreader informed her. 'In an overnight sensation, allegations have been made in a Philippines newspaper that Taggart murdered a barmaid in a popular tourist resort in Manila last May.'

Jen's glass of orange juice crashed to the floor.

Murder?

No! her mind screamed.

That one ghastly word smote her like a knife thrust. Hands over her mouth, she watched the screen in sick horror. Harry was backing towards the front steps of Polly's house, shaking his head and clearly refusing to comment. A rather beefy journalist lunged forward with a microphone and seemed to make a grab for Harry.

During the scuffle that followed the cameraman lost control momentarily and the picture dipped towards the ground, missing some of the action, then was righted again, showing Jen a distorted angle of Harry's angry face and his raised hand and, just before the camera image faded, there was a full screen shot of the beefy journalist flying backwards into Polly's rose garden.

This can't be happening. It can't. There has to be a mistake.

The news broadcast moved on to a different story while Jen sat in numbed horror, unable to take in what she'd just seen.

Murder? Again, her mind shouted, No!

She'd sensed an element of danger in Harry, but never this...

It had to be a mistake. It had to be. Harry couldn't have committed murder.

Could he? For a sickening moment she allowed herself to imagine it was true. She pictured him with a gun, a knife, a raised, angry fist... No! *No! No!*

She remembered the other night when he'd turned up on her doorstep with the bottle of wine. *You can't hold me up on your doorstep like I've committed a capital offence...* Surely he couldn't have said that if he really had committed a crime?

She'd looked into his eyes, she'd kissed him. She'd trusted him with Millicent. He might look like a bad boy and act like a playboy, he might write bloodthirsty thrillers full of danger and intrigue, but he was a good man at heart.

He'd cared about Millicent.

And last night...he'd been hot with desire and she'd been vulnerable and yet he'd walked away rather than hurt her...

Slowly this realisation sank in and she began to feel a little calmer. She couldn't accept this accusation. She wouldn't.

Depressing the button on the remote control, she reached for her phone instead. 'Cleo,' she said in response to a greeting from the office answering machine. 'It's Jen here. I have an important meeting with a client first thing, so I'm going straight there and won't be in till later this morning.'

Snatching up her suit jacket and briefcase, she stepped over the smashed glass and spilled juice and hurried out of the house.

'You're in deep trouble,' Harry's agent, Reg Walker, barked into the phone.

'I'm not, I'm innocent,' Harry growled. He was taking the call on his mobile phone in Polly's front room, lounging back in an armchair with an ankle crossing a knee, trying to stay calm while his stomach squirmed worse than a bucket of worms. 'What about the old saying that there's no such thing as bad publicity?'

'Having allegations like this thrown at you is taking publicity a little too far, mate.'

'But I've just told you I'm innocent. It's a beat up story in a second-rate rag, for heaven's sake.'

'Yeah…but until you've been cleared I'm nervous and your publishers are nervous. I've had Jarrod Eagle on the phone chewing my ear, making threats about turning down the proposal for your next book.'

'You're joking.' Sweat filmed Harry's brow and his throat constricted on a clot of anger mixed with the first stirrings of fear.

'Eagle wants this resolved. Fast,' said Reg. 'And he claims you're on your own with it, Harry. He's seen how you—ah—*handled*, maybe I should say *manhandled* the press this morning and he's not interested in providing you with PR backup.'

Harry scowled at the toe of his boot and refrained from commenting.

'But if I were you,' Reg went on, 'I'd be doing everything I could to put this bloody bushfire out.'

'Yeah and how exactly do I fight scandal like this? What do you advise? Can we sue them or something?'

There was an uncomfortably long pause. 'I'll ask around, mate, but to tell you the truth, in my twenty years as an agent I haven't come across anything like this. In terms of disasters this one's gold-plated. I'll be honest and say I wouldn't know where to start.'

In other words, he couldn't count on Reg at all.

'Great.' Harry ground the word out. What a mess. He was fast losing patience with his agent, his publishers, with the whole damn world. 'Well…I guess I'll get back to you when I have some good news.'

As he disconnected a knock rapped at the front door and he stiffened, instinctively preparing for another wretched twist to this rotten morning. What next? What other catastrophe awaited him? He heard Polly's light footsteps as she hurried down the hall to answer the knock and he strained to hear who the caller was but the voices were too low.

Rolling his shoulders, he tried to relax and he slumped into the chair, letting his head fall back and closing his eyes. He'd never felt so angry or so helpless. This disaster was so unjust. But he didn't even have time to wallow in self-pity. He had a battle on his hands. He had to think clearly. It was important that he allowed his mind to find a clear path through this nightmare.

'Morning, Harry.'

His eyes whipped open. 'Jen!' He hadn't heard her come into the room and his heart punched hard as he sprang to his feet. 'What are you doing here?'

Her mouth tilted into a weak, half-smile. 'I got the crazy impression you were having a publicity crisis.'

'Well, yeah—but you don't want to get mixed up in it.'

'Why not?' she asked, regarding him with a steady, frowning stare.

Holding out his hands palms up in a gesture of helplessness, he shook his head. 'This is heavy stuff. It's out of your league.'

'That's for me to decide,' she said and, with the haughty composure of a model on a cat-walk, she swung the strap of a soft leather briefcase from her shoulder, slipped into a chair opposite him and slowly crossed her slim legs. 'You don't know what league I can play in.'

A challenging light sparkled in her eyes as she tucked a silky, straight strand of hair behind one neat, pink ear.

She was wearing her dark pinstriped suit and looked immaculately groomed and totally businesslike—although her legs in their silky stockings and her neat high-heeled pumps were a sexy distraction. She was paler than usual and delicate shadows underlined her eyes. Had her night been as sleepless as his? Could she really be as calm as she made out?

'As far as I know I'm still your publicity agent,' she said.

'Well, the jury's still out on that,' he confessed. 'I'm not in the best position to wield influence with Eagle and Browne right now, so I haven't been able to keep my promise this morning.'

'It doesn't matter.'

'Looks like both our jobs are at risk,' he said.

'So we'll just have to rescue ourselves, right?'

He was still standing in the middle of the room, transfixed by her cool sang-froid. His stomach clenched as she picked up the copy of *The Gazette* that lay on the coffee table and turned it to page three and the oversized photo of him kissing Lisa at the theatre two nights ago.

'We have a PR crisis and it's what I'm trained to take care of,' she said. 'I'm the best person to handle your problem.'

'You'd be crazy to get involved, Jen.'

'Most people tell me I'm excessively sane.'

'But I've been accused of—' He couldn't bring himself to say the word in her presence. She was Jen—sweet, generous, modest, essentially good in every way. Not that he needed to say anything. The thick black headline accompanying the photo announced it to the world: *Playboy Author Linked with Murder*.

Her level, unflinching gaze held his as she dropped the paper back on to the table. 'You haven't been officially accused of anything,' she said. 'These are merely scandalous allegations. Anyone who knew you would know they were rubbish.'

For a moment he was overcome by her faith in him, but his relief and gratitude were short-lived. Jen had no idea what she was buying into here. For crying out loud, she organised tea parties for bookshops. 'Jen, why would you want to do this?'

She shrugged. 'You've been a great help to me. One good turn deserves another.'

'If you're here because you think you're in l—' He bit back the word.

Jen jerked her gaze from his as colour flooded her cheeks and Harry cursed himself for being so blunt.

'What I told you last night is irrelevant,' she said. 'I'm here because you need my expertise. I'm a public relations consultant and this is a publicity matter.' Throwing back her shoulders, she took a deep breath and let it out slowly. 'We have to put personal considerations aside and be totally professional,' she said.

'Why don't those journalists try being professional?' Harry cried. 'How can their papers just fling crazy accusations like that?'

'It's wrong,' Jen agreed. 'But it's happened. The thing is, fighting back with your fists is not going to help.'

'So what am I supposed to do?'

'Stop pacing, Harry. Sit down and I'll explain.'

For a full five seconds he stared at her stern, determined face, then he lowered himself back into his chair. Surprise didn't go halfway to describing how he felt right now. Who would

have guessed that such a shy, blushing, bash-
ful girl could be so level-headed and confident
in a crisis?

She uncrossed her legs with graceful ease
and leaned forward. 'I understand that this situation is very, very serious for you, but we
mustn't let that throw us. We have to look at
this as a standard crisis—a media issue. That
way we can treat it as we would *any* crisis
and there are steps in damage control that we
can take.'

'There are?'

'Absolutely. I can take you through this one
step at a time, Harry. I can help.'

He sat back without commenting and let her
continue.

'For example,' she said, 'you need to start
with total disclosure—transparency. That
means laying all your cards on the table and
telling the whole story. Are you prepared to
do that?'

'Sure.'

'Warts and all? If you don't, it will come
out in the end anyhow.'

He frowned. 'Sounds like I need a lawyer.'

'Not yet. As I said, at the moment this is simply a media issue.' She picked up *The Gazette* again. 'This paper is noted for its scandalmongering and the report is biased and unbalanced.'

'Of course it is. They ran the story without even trying to contact me to get my side.'

Jen nodded. 'And all the media people will know that but, unfortunately, they're sharks hungry for blood. I just want to make sure it's not your blood.'

'That's what's really thrown me. I thought I had a good relationship with the press. You saw how they loved me at the book launch. I enjoyed dealing with them.'

She nodded, smiling in sympathy. 'I know. But they're a fickle lot. They can adore you one week and ruin you a week later. That's why you have to handle them carefully. If you front the media behind a lawyer they'll think you're preparing for a court appeal and that's not going to happen because you're innocent, aren't you?'

'Of course.' His clipped reply sounded more impatient than he'd meant it to. 'The only correct fact in that entire story was that I managed the Sundowner Bar in the Philippines for two months.'

He watched the way her hair fell in a silky curtain as she unzipped her briefcase and took out a notepad and pen. 'So can you tell me your version of this story now? In a nutshell?'

'Are you going to tuck your hair behind your ear again?'

'What?' Jen's face flamed bright red.

'I'm sorry. It's just so neat the way you do that.'

Her cheeks stayed pink as she pursed her lips like a cranky schoolmarm. 'Your story, Harry.'

He leaned forward and rested his elbows on his knees with his hands in front of him, fingers steepled. 'In a nutshell…OK…' The last thing he wanted to do with Jen was talk about this, but he had no choice. 'The poor woman who died, Maria Deltante, was a good friend. Just a *friend*,' he added when he saw the look in Jen's eyes. 'She was an honest, hard-working barmaid and she was killed because of her courage, because she resisted pressure from criminals involved in stand over tactics and drug running.'

He grimaced. 'I found out what was happening and tried to intervene, but unfortunately I wasn't quick enough to save Maria.'

'Will the police in Manila be able to vouch for you?'

'Sure. In fact, they warned me that I wasn't safe any more and got me out of the country.' He shrugged. 'I'd be willing to bet that the person laying blame at my feet now is a member of that same crime ring, someone trying to discredit my evidence by diverting attention away from the real perpetrators.'

Jen nodded grimly as she finished making notes. 'OK. I'll have to put through a few phone calls to Manila, but we need to convene a press conference as soon as possible.' She sent him an encouraging smile. 'You need a chance to talk to the journalists on *your* terms. We want to get the media to run your story and not just responses to someone else's wild claims.'

'That would certainly help matters.'

'And you'll have to create credibility.' As she spoke she stabbed the padded arm of her chair with the end of her pen as if to underscore her points. 'You're going to have to explain your actions on your doorstep this morning. Apologise to the bloke who ended up in Polly's rose-bed.'

'Like hell.'

'Like you mean it, Harry. Whatever you do, you mustn't blame the media.'

'If you insist,' he muttered through gritted teeth.

Jen rose. Her smile was a mixture of encouragement and concern laced with something deeper that tugged at Harry's heart and made him want to howl like a mournful wolf. He jumped to his feet.

'Switch off your mobile phone and stay here for now,' she told him. 'Don't speak to any more journalists until the conference. I've already primed Polly to answer all your calls.

I don't want anyone ambushing you to get an exclusive. And I'll send a car for you.'

She forced a wry grin. 'This is definitely one time when you should not be driving. I'll probably have to sneak you into the hotel by a back entrance.'

He almost cracked a smile. 'I'd be looking forward to it if it wasn't so damn serious.'

Abruptly she crossed the room towards him and stood on tiptoes to kiss him lightly on the cheek and he felt the soft warmth of her lips, the silky swish of her hair on his skin.

He reached for her hand and cradled it in both of his. 'Thanks, Jen. I don't know that I deserve your faith, but thanks. It means a great deal.'

She drew in a sharp breath and he saw two bright spots of colour appear in her cheeks. 'Do what I tell you and we'll have this nailed by this evening.'

Then, as if she'd been jolted by electricity, she pulled away from him, turned and hurried out of the room, and Harry was left alone with no more than a trace of perfume as fresh as an apple orchard on a spring morning.

CHAPTER TEN

HARRY was nervous. Jen could tell by the quick, tight smile he flashed over his audience. Although he didn't glance towards her as she sat to one side of the conference room, she nodded, smiling her encouragement while her hands reached for the sides of her chair and gripped them hard.

Thank heavens he had no idea that she'd never handled anything as serious or as complex as his problem, or that she was even more nervous than he was. If this press conference failed Harry's reputation and his career could be in tatters, not to mention her own.

But for the most part her job was over. It was in Harry's hands now. One of her biggest challenges had been hiding her worry from him, persuading him that she knew how to manage a crisis, even though she'd been working from a dimly remembered lecture she'd once heard at a seminar.

Don't look down and you won't fall. It was a mantra she'd been repeating all day and she whispered it again now as Harry cleared his throat and launched into his campaign.

'Thanks for coming, folks. Jen Summers tells me it's OK to be totally honest with all of you. Open and transparent, she says. But, before I go too far, I should explain my behaviour this morning and offer some apologies...'

He paused for a moment, letting his gaze take in the assembled crowd, then he shook his head and his mouth quirked into a rueful, one-sided grin. 'I staggered out half-asleep this morning and ran into you lot in attack mode. A pack of hard-nosed Australian journalists armed and dangerous with microphones. That's enough to panic even the toughest character in my books.'

There was a rustle of reaction. Jen held her breath as Harry smiled again and gestured to the journalist who'd ended up in Polly's rose-bed. 'I'm sorry about what happened this morning, mate, but, to be honest, I'm more concerned that I could have sent the wrong message to you. I have nothing to hide…

'This is all about the killers of my friend being brought to justice,' Harry said, standing proudly now, facing the crowded room with his broad shoulders squared and his jaw firm, just like the warrior who strode fearlessly into the press conference in Maurice's salon.

Oh, Lord, she loved him.

'This is about you people doing your job and telling the public here and in the Philippines what's really going on.'

Although she couldn't relax Jen could sense that Harry was growing more sure, more convincing, with each word. His strong presence and his rich, dark chocolate voice were working their magic. The restless pack of journalists stopped fidgeting and began to listen hard, their pens racing, the cameras humming.

They would be firing their questions soon, but the tide was turning…

* * *

By the time it was over she was completely exhausted, flattened by the kind of hollow, shivery tiredness that follows a long and arduous battle.

Beside her Harry removed his jacket, loosened his shirt collar and tie and sprawled back in his chair with his legs extended away from him and his arms hanging loosely at his sides. He looked as whacked as she felt.

Was it really only this morning that she'd turned on her television and seen him on Polly's lawn? She realised suddenly that she hadn't eaten anything all day. She'd been too sick with fear.

His gaze slid slowly towards her and he cocked a dark eyebrow, then winked at her, sending her a tired grin. 'We did it,' he said. 'We sent them away happy.'

She nodded. '*You* did it, Harry. You hit exactly the right note and you convinced them. You were magnificent and you even had *The Gazette* eating out of your hand. Congratulations, you really turned this around.'

She closed her eyes against a wave of nausea. It was only now, after they'd reached a safe conclusion to a horrendously long and busy ordeal, that she realised how truly tense and terrified she'd been.

'Jen, you were the amazing one.' Harry's voice sounded soft and low next to her ear. 'How can I thank you?'

She opened her eyes to find him squatting beside her, his grey gaze level with hers.

'This morning I was a drowning man. You threw me a life-belt.'

Her heart galloped as she saw unmistakable tenderness in his eloquent face. Her body grew tight and hot at finding him so suddenly close. Kissing close.

Her eyes travelled over him hungrily, drinking in loving details—the curly lock of dark hair falling on to his forehead, the silky length of his thick, black lashes and the sea-water clarity of his grey eyes, the tan of his skin and the manly shadow of new beard darkening his jaw, the crooked tilt of his smile and the gorgeous lushness of his lips.

Her pulse points beat wildly and she couldn't stop her own lips from parting in silent invitation. If Harry kissed her now, she might swoon…literally…she might sink to the floor…

With one finger, he tucked a strand of her hair behind her ear. 'You look done in,' he said gently. 'Let me buy you dinner.'

She gulped back her disappointment. Of course he wasn't going to kiss her. Not after the way she'd sent him packing last night. Despite the battle they'd waged side by side today nothing else had changed. Nothing.

Slowly she shook her head. 'Thanks, but I don't think I could eat a thing right now.'

It was ironic that she felt even closer to Harry now. They'd made a great team and yet this was the end.

Very soon they would be going their own separate ways.

'We should be celebrating,' he said, but, like her, he looked tired, not in a party mood. 'Can I get you a drink? Anything? I owe you so much.'

She smiled. 'If this turns out well you can put in a good word about me to your publishers.'

He looked stricken. 'Of course—that goes without saying.' His hand closed over hers where it lay in her lap and she watched with fascination as his broad thumb stroked her skin. Looking up, she saw muscles working in his throat. 'You're incredibly special,' he murmured. 'I've never known a girl quite like you. I've never met anyone who made me feel better.'

She felt suddenly fragile, like a very delicate specimen of newly blown glassware— glowing hot, suspended in the moment between melting back to nothing, or growing strong and solid and beautiful.

If Harry Ryder loved her she could be as strong and beautiful as a mountain.

He released her hand and rose to his feet, letting out a long, pained sigh, and her hopes collapsed. What a silly fool she was. The depth of feeling that burned in Harry's gaze was gratitude. He was thankful that she'd saved his career. He didn't love her. No amount of gratitude added up to love. How could she have forgotten that, even for a moment? Harry enjoyed a little light flirtation but he could never return her deep feelings.

He stood beside her, looking down, unaware of the pain he'd just caused. 'I'll be heading off soon but can I write to you?'

Struggling to her feet, she blinked, determined to hide her despair. 'From Hong Kong?'

'Yeah.'

'I don't think you should write.'

He frowned. 'Why not? We're friends, aren't we? I'd like to stay in touch. You never know, when I come back, maybe we can pick up from here...'

Not if she was to get on with her life. She needed to forget about him. Make a clean break. 'I'm not much good with letters. Mine sound more like shopping lists or, at best, news bulletins.'

'That's OK,' he said. 'I'm a writer—I love writing letters.' He lifted a hand to touch her again, but seemed to have second thoughts and left it hovering in mid-air before letting it fall to his side once more. His eyes shimmered and he smiled nervously. 'Sometimes I can find a way to say things on paper that I can't get out in conversation.'

Jen couldn't smile, so she grimaced instead. 'I'm sure you write wonderful letters, H R Taggart, but...*please*...save them for Polly... or...or for your parents.' She hurried away from him, moving along the table, gathering up the leftover press releases and shoving them haphazardly into her briefcase.

She refused to look Harry's way but she sensed his impatience and felt the vibration of his fingers drumming the table top.

'I'll probably write the letters anyway,' he said at last.

'Suit yourself,' she said, knowing she sounded petulant, but too miserable to care.

His footsteps approached. 'Jen, we've had a huge day. We've had a terrific victory. I owe you everything. Don't let's part like this.'

'How else can we part, Harry?' Her voice was shrill but she couldn't help it. She was falling apart inside. 'What more do you want from me?'

Their eyes met and an unspoken, tortured, inadequate message passed between them.

'I don't know,' he said at last. He offered a half-smile, lifting his hands and shrugging helplessly. 'I honestly don't know, Jen, but I'll write just the same.'

CHAPTER ELEVEN

HARRY'S letters came regularly for six weeks and then stopped.

They arrived in blue airmail envelopes addressed in bold, black handwriting, bearing bright stamps showing scenes of Chinese junks with tan sails billowing as they cruised on Hong Kong's harbour. Each time Jen spied a patch of blue through the slit in her letter box her heart leapt. Most times the envelopes were fat with what she guessed were long, newsy letters.

But she didn't read them.

Oh, her fingers itched to slit the fine paper, to devour Harry's messages, but instead she forced herself to place each letter unopened in a shoe box in the bottom of her wardrobe and then she dumped a tangle of old boots and tennis shoes on top and tried to forget about them. About Harry.

During the day at work it was business as usual. Harry's publishers withdrew their complaint about Jen and her boss came back from her holiday and complimented her on how well she'd managed in her absence.

In the various media outlets Harry's name was totally cleared. Three weeks after he left, *The Gazette* reported that three men had been arrested in Manila and the Public Prosecutor praised Harry's role in providing important evidence.

Christmas came and went and when Jen gathered with her family for the traditional festivities a deliriously excited Lisa told her that she and Michael Wolfe were getting married. On New Year's Eve Jen went to a party at Lisa's place and listened to the couple's ecstatic plans to spend half their time in London and half in Australia.

She was very, very happy for Lisa, for Michael, but most of all for Millicent.

'Isn't my Daddy wonderful?' the little girl asked Jen at least ten times during the evening and Jen agreed. She was thrilled by the bright, ecstatic joy shining in her niece's eyes, even though it made her more aware than ever of everything she'd lost when Harry left.

Home alone, she decided to begin the new year by redecorating, starting with the sun room at the back of the house. She spent hours poring over decorating magazines, paint charts and books of fabric samples, trying to decide whether she wanted to give the room a traditional, cottagey look, or if she should turn it into something very bright and bold, or something muted, minimalist and contemporary.

The important thing was to keep occupied. If she kept busy enough, she decided, she would get over Harry. And, strangely, while Harry's letters kept arriving promptly every week she felt OK. Edgy and curious, fretful and lonely, but OK. Just.

It was only when the letters stopped that she fell in a heap. It was as if their constant dropping into her letter box had been like an inoculation, keeping her immune from the worst of her pain, but once they ceased coming the protection vanished.

Of course, she couldn't blame Harry for giving up. She hadn't once replied to anything he'd sent. But she couldn't help worrying. Had something happened? Was he hurt? Sick? Had the inevitable happened? Had his overwhelming gratitude diminished with time? Had he found another more interesting, sexier woman?

To her horror she realised that she was more miserable and heartsick than ever. She loved Harry even more in his absence than she had when he was close by. At night she lay hugging her pillow, torturing herself with memories of his laughter, his kisses, his random acts of kindness towards Millicent. Over and over she relived the sheer exhilaration of being involved with such an exciting man.

After another two weeks without a letter she broke down.

Fear more than curiosity sent her to her knees, scrambling to retrieve the letters from the dusty box at the bottom of the wardrobe. Her hands shook as she carried them to her bed and set them out in order on her white chenille bedspread. She noticed that the last letter was the thinnest. No doubt it held the clue to Harry's sudden silence.

Appalled by how ill she felt, she reached into a drawer in her bedside table for a nail file and used it to slit the envelope carefully open. Inside there was a single sheet of paper. She held her breath as she unfolded it.

Kowloon
January 6th

Dear Jen,

This is the last letter I will write to you. Over the past six weeks I've exposed my innermost thoughts to you in ways I've never dared with any other woman—or any other person, for that matter. But my efforts to share with you what I've discovered about myself since I left Brisbane haven't been enough.

It seems ironic that I can move my readers with fiction and fantasy but I can't reach you with genuine, sincere expressions of love.

Love? Jen felt a harrowing flash, half-alarm and half-joy. She felt so suddenly overcome the paper shook in her hands as she read on.

I was tempted to stop writing after I received no reply to my first two letters. But I clung to my belief that the written word is important and I just had to keep telling you how I felt.

You might wonder why I didn't just pick up the phone and ring you, but when I speak I don't necessarily say what lies in my heart. That comes most clearly when I write.

You've no idea how I laboured. I spent days preparing the letter that listed my many reasons for loving you. I was sure I'd outstripped the efforts of the most ardent poet. But you weren't moved.

Last week I laid my heart bare and begged you to marry me, to make me a happy man.

Your continued silence is my answer.

So be it. I can do no more. I never

dreamed that unrequited love could be so painful. I guess this is part of my education, but I'm afraid I can't be grateful.

Of course there is the chance that you haven't read my letters. If that's the case, your opinion of me must be so poor that my cause must still be abandoned.

I'm leaving Hong Kong tomorrow but I won't bother giving you a forwarding address. Not much point, is there? Take care.

Always,

Harry.

Jen collapsed on to her bed in an agony of tears.

What had she done? How could she have been so stupid? Stupid, stupid, stupid!

In the scant minutes she'd spent reading the letter her heart had leapt, raced with joy and then plunged to the darkest depths of despair. Harry loved her. He wanted to *marry* her! And now it was too late. Oh, God, she'd thrown his heartfelt expressions of love into the bottom of her wardrobe!

'I didn't know,' she sobbed, curling into a ball of misery and hugging her knees. 'Oh, Harry, I didn't know!'

Hot tears streamed down her face and her throat burned and stung with the build-up of a further flood of tears. Her horrified heart felt leaden. She could feel its awful weight sinking like a heavy stone in the centre of her chest. She felt so foolish, so anguished, so filled with remorse she wanted to drop off the edge of the world.

Surely there could be no punishment savage enough for her stupidity. How could she have ignored Harry's letters? Why hadn't she guessed?

And now he was gone… *I won't bother giving you a forwarding address.*

She lay in a stupefied daze, staring at the scattering of blue envelopes on her white bedspread. Why hadn't she ever noticed how bright and hopeful they looked with their bold handwritten addresses and colourful stamps? Now they seemed to mock her. Inside those sealed squares of flimsy paper lay so many precious secrets. Could she bear to open them now?

As she lay huddled in pain shadows crept into the room and she turned on a bedside lamp. Eventually, in the little puddle of yellow light, she picked up the first letter and slit it open. She read them all in order from the first jaunty but impersonal descriptions of Hong Kong through the progression of personal insights to the deeply private, beautifully perfect expressions of love.

There it was on paper. The most incredibly moving account of Harry's growing awareness of his feelings for her.

In his third letter, he'd written:

I was walking on the beach at Repulse Bay today and I found a shell. It was only a small, rather ordinary little shell. Pinkish-brown, edged with white, with a smooth delicate tawny underside. As I held it in my hand and admired its neat ridges, its perfect roundness and stunning simplicity, I thought of you. I ached for you.

And I understood how exceptionally rare you are. You have a quiet, natural beauty that is so easily overlooked because it's not showy or ostentatious. These days, I love all shades of brown. Brown is my favourite colour…

In another letter he told her that the Philippines issue was settled:

I owe you too much. At least the road is cleared now…

And yet another time he said:

You asked me once what I was frightened of and I wouldn't tell you, but I'll admit now that I was afraid of you. You see, Jen, I think I sensed right from the start that I could too easily fall in love with you. There was something about you, your home, your generous heart and your quiet but winsome charm that reached out and touched me deeply. You are everything that I am not. You are the part of myself that I could never find.

But I fought against this knowledge. I was running away from commitment. I crave it now. When I think of you, Jen, I think of lasting happiness.

It was quite dark by the time Jen read all the letters through twice. There were times when Harry's words made her so exquisitely happy she had to stop to give a little thrilled squeak of joy, hugging the paper to her chest, but then she would remember that through her own silly fault she might never see him again and she was plunged back into the blackest misery.

If only she'd given Harry a chance to talk all this through before he left. *Idiot.* She groaned aloud as she remembered how he'd tried to tell her that his feelings were changing, how he could express his feelings better in writing. *Imbecile.* She'd never had the confidence to believe that a man like Harry could love such an ordinary girl as herself. She'd been too certain that the end result would be more disappointment.

Foolish wimp. She had disappointment in spades now.

Lying on her bed, wretched and despairing, she thought about ringing Polly McLean to ask her if she knew how to find Harry, but her courage faltered and she decided to try her friend Camille in Mullinjim first.

'I don't suppose Jonno's heard from Harry Ryder recently?' she asked Camille, trying to sound casual.

'Not for a few weeks,' Camille told her. 'Actually, Jonno mentioned Harry at breakfast only this morning. He was wondering where he'd got to. The last thing he heard Harry was leaving Hong Kong, but he never indicated where.'

There was an awkward pause while Jen held her breath to stop herself from blubbering into the phone.

'I'm sorry I can't be more help,' Camille said.

'Oh, it's OK.' Jen sounded squeaky. 'I was only calling on the off-chance.'

'You don't have to pretend to me, honey. I know heartache when I hear it. It's not OK that you can't find Harry, is it?'

'No,' Jen wailed. And then she couldn't hold back any longer. 'I'm desperately in love with him.'

'Oh, Jen, I'm so sorry. Men can be insensitive brutes, can't they?'

Jen sniffed. 'It's not Harry's fault. I feel so awful. I'm the one who's been insensitive.'

'How? What's happened?'

'Harry wrote me the most beautiful letters and told me he loves me and I didn't read them till it was too late and now he's gone and I've lost him, Camille. I've lost him.'

'Say that again. Did he actually write to tell you he loves you?'

'Yes!'

'And he wants to *marry* you?'

'Yes,' Jen sobbed.

'Wow, that's wonderful! It's amazing! Goodness, from the rumours I've heard it's a miracle. Harry's supposed to have been terribly reluctant to commit.'

'I know,' Jen cried. 'But he said he wants to get married, and now he's gone off somewhere and he thinks I don't care.'

'Oh, darling. He won't stay away for ever. I'm sure you'll find him. I promise we'll let you know the minute we hear anything.'

'Thanks, Camille.'

'I'll be thinking of you, Jen.'

'Thanks, I—I've got to go.' Dropping the receiver quickly, Jen shoved her fist hard against her mouth, but that couldn't stop the tears from streaming down her cheeks.

She made a cup of tea and drank it slowly and then tried to quieten her thoughts by taking a warm bath with scented oils before she made the call to Polly McLean.

'Oh, Jen, my dear girl.' Harry's grandmother sounded quite distressed. 'I was hoping *you* could tell *me* where Harry is now. None of his family knows. It's as if he doesn't want to be found.'

'Oh.' An explosion of panic ricocheted through her. 'He wouldn't have done anything *foolish*, would he?'

'Quite possibly,' Polly said, but when she heard Jen's horrified gasp she added hastily, 'I was being facetious, Jen. I don't think he's come to any real harm. Don't worry, dear. We're used to Harry's sudden disappearances. He'll turn up again when he's good and ready. But he shouldn't be putting you through this anxiety. You don't deserve it.'

'Oh, but I do,' Jen cried. 'I'm afraid I've hurt him.'

Polly was silent for a moment and then she surprised Jen by saying, 'That's the best news I've heard in ages.'

The cryptic comment made no sense. Polly adored Harry. 'What on earth do you mean?'

'I mean have faith, Jen. I think this dilemma might have a happy ending.'

But Jen felt worse than ever.

Next morning, in desperation, she rang Harry's publishers, Eagle and Browne.

'Sorry,' she was told. 'Harry sent in his completed manuscript and now he's in one of his drifting moods. They strike from time to time.' The only help they could offer was his grandmother's address.

She'd hit a brick wall.

CHAPTER TWELVE

TOWARDS the end of January, the week before Australia Day, Lisa telephoned Jen. 'Come and stay with us for the long weekend,' she said. 'Michael and I have bought a new apartment. You'll love it. It's right on the beachfront at Sunshine Beach and there are sea views from every room. Say you'll come, Jen. We won't accept any excuses.'

Jen was surprised at the pleading edge in her sister's voice, but she didn't really need much persuading. She certainly didn't want to spend a long lonely weekend on her own and she loved the beach. Besides, a good vigorous swim in the surf might shake out some of her misery.

'Thanks,' she said. 'I'd love to come.'

That settled, they chatted briefly about Millicent and the phenomenal progress she'd made on the violin since Michael had come into her life.

As they were about to hang up Jen said quickly, 'Lisa, I need to ask you something.'

'Ask away,' Lisa said, but she sounded cautious.

'I can't help being curious about you and Michael.'

There was a soft sigh, almost of relief, on the other end of the phone.

'You don't mind my asking, do you?' Jen said.

'No. What do you want to know?'

'You've never explained what the problem was between you two—or—or how you reconciled whatever it was that kept you apart.'

'Well…it's rather an incredible story,' Lisa said. 'I couldn't believe it when I got to the bottom of our problem. Can you imagine that a brilliant, gorgeous man like Michael could have doubts about whether he was good enough for me?'

Jen gulped. 'I guess…not.'

'Me?' Lisa cried. 'I'm nothing but a clothes horse, while Michael's clever and funny and sexy and so-o-o-o talented... And yet he didn't think he was good-looking or exciting enough! He thought I would want to marry someone incredibly handsome like a movie star. Can you believe that?'

'Yes,' Jen whispered. Of course she could. These were the very same fears she'd erected between herself and Harry.

'Michael is the only man I've ever loved,' Lisa said, her voice warming prettily. 'Thank heavens Millicent and I were able to convince him. With a little help from Harry,' she added, almost as an afterthought. 'Harry's appearance at Millicent's recital and then at the theatre drove poor Michael to the limits of his tolerance.'

'I'm so happy it's all worked out for you,' Jen said.

'So am I, little sis. Believe me, so am I.'

Jen left for the coast straight after work on Friday afternoon and her spirits began to lift almost as soon as she turned north on to the highway. The traffic was heavy with thousands of holidaymakers grabbing the last chance for a weekend of sun and surf before the school year started, but she turned on the radio and adjusted the air-conditioning and before long the suburbs were giving way to pine forests and then the Glass House Mountains. Her excitement mounted as she anticipated her first glimpse of the sparkling blue of the Pacific.

The weather was warm, but not too hot, and there was no sign of rain. It was going to be a wonderful weekend. That thought sustained her as she steered her little Volkswagen up the magnificent steep driveway to the rather grand apartment block and greeted her sister. Arm in arm, they climbed the stone steps to Lisa's beautiful penthouse.

And almost immediately she heard the voice.

Deep, masculine, rumbling. Mellow. A dark chocolate voice.

Hairs rose on the back of her neck and her chest squeezed so tightly she couldn't breathe. *Harry?* It couldn't be him. She stared at Lisa. 'Why didn't you warn me?'

'Warn you? What about?' Lisa frowned as if she didn't understand, but there was a wary flash in her green eyes that didn't fool Jen.

'Harry's here, isn't he?'

Lisa's eyes widened but she kept her smile bland. 'Yes. He's upstairs with Michael.'

'How? Why?' Jen cried. 'I don't understand. What's he doing here?'

'Harry and Michael met up in Hong Kong. Michael's concert tour took him there and the two of them really hit it off. They went on to Beijing together. They're great mates now.'

'I—I didn't know Harry was back in Australia,' Jen said, lowering her voice and casting frantic glances in the direction of the spiral staircase leading to the next level, wanting to dash up those stairs and find him, but frightened, too. What if he was so angry with her he didn't want to see her again?

She was distracted from these thoughts by a small Millicent-shaped missile that came rushing towards her and hugged her hips. 'Auntie Jen!'

'Hello, darling.' Jen bent low to return the hug. Millicent was dressed in her swimsuit and smelled of sunscreen lotion and salt water. In the past Jen had loved those smells. They conjured instant happy images of summer holidays, sun and fun in the surf. But now she felt dizzy and ill.

'Harry's here,' Millicent announced excitedly.

'Yes,' Jen said, but she couldn't bring herself to make further comment. Looking over Millicent's shoulder, she saw a girl of about twenty.

'This is Annie, my new nanny,' Millicent said, giggling over the rhyme.

Annie the nanny was blonde and very pretty in a healthy, suntanned, outdoorsy way and, like Millicent, she was wearing a swimsuit, only hers was a pink bikini covered by a thin, see-through cheesecloth shirt.

'Hi, Annie,' Jen said, feeling ashamed that her first thought was to wonder if Harry had been impressed by the nanny's prettiness.

'Millicent, run and tell Daddy that Jen's here,' said Lisa. 'Come on, Jen, I'll show you to your room and then you can join us on the roof for a pre-dinner drink. You'll love the rooftop garden.'

Jen's heart pounded as she followed Lisa across the expanse of polished timber floor to a bedroom facing the sea.

She set her overnight bag beside the bed. The blinds were drawn back and the huge floor to ceiling windows provided a stunning vista of the spectacular sweep of coastline.

'Oh, this is gorgeous,' she said. 'What a fantastic view!' But her response was automatic. Views of sparkling white sand and sapphire blue ocean paled into insignificance beside the thought that Harry was here in this house.

Her stomach was plunging and her heart was knocking in her throat. She looked at

Lisa. 'Does Harry know I'm coming here for the weekend?'

'Michael may have mentioned it,' her sister said evasively, not quite meeting Jen's direct gaze.

'Did he—did he say anything about me?'

'Nothing bad.' Lisa seemed eager to change the subject. She pointed to a door in the wall. 'There's a tiny *en suite* bathroom through there so, as soon as you've freshened up, hurry upstairs to join us.'

'Do you think I should change into different clothes?'

Lisa sent a quick glance over Jen's simple ginger and white spotted sun-dress. 'No,' she said. 'That little dress shows off your olive skin beautifully. I wish I didn't burn so easily. I have to stay covered up whenever I'm in the sun.'

As Jen splashed cold water on her face and brushed her hair she felt sick with apprehension. The thought of seeing Harry filled her with trembling expectation, but she didn't know whether to be happy or worried. Was he angry with her for not answering his letters? Was he hurt? Bitter? *Over* her?

Her knees knocked against each other as she climbed the stairs leading to the rooftop garden. The setting was, as she'd expected, beautiful—pale terracotta tiles, potted palms and lush, colourful tropical shrubs, tubs spilling with bright bougainvillea and, overhead, the wide blue sky turning pink and mauve as the afternoon slipped towards evening.

All this she saw in a split second.

And then she saw Harry.

He was standing with his back to the wrought iron railing that bordered the rooftop. His light cotton shirt was open at the neck, its long sleeves rolled back to the elbows. A breeze made the shirt billow and the collar flapped against the back of his neck.

Beside him stood a glass-topped outdoor table surrounded by wicker chairs. On the table was an ice bucket holding a bottle of wine and wineglasses and a platter of antipasto, but there was no sign of Lisa and Michael, or Millicent and Annie.

All her feelings for him came in a hot, sweet rush and her first impulse was to do everything at once—run to him, throw her arms around him and tell him how sorry she was that she hadn't replied to his letters. She needed to explain why she hadn't read his letters, had to tell him she loved him.

But his face was an expressionless mask and she was held back by confusion, frozen by too many questions.

She had no idea how he was feeling now, how low his opinion of her might be. His expression was so deadpan it scared her.

Only one thought remained clear and fixed in her mind. She couldn't wimp out this time. She couldn't turn and run. Whatever Harry had to say, she had to hear it.

Her legs threatened to buckle beneath her, but she forced herself to walk towards him.

He watched her progress, his eyes coldly serious beneath dark brows. He was more tanned than she remembered but his face seemed a little thinner so that his cheekbones were more prominent. Rays from the sinking sun lit his hair, giving the curling edges a gilded sheen.

'Hello, Harry,' she said when she reached him.

'Hi,' he said, without smiling.

Jen struggled to breathe. 'Where are the others?'

'Michael said something about seeing a man about a cello and they vanished.'

Jen gave a little shrug and her hands flapped against her thighs. 'So it—it seems that my sister and Michael may have been conspiring to bring us together.'

'Who knows?' He shrugged and then frowned. 'This wasn't my idea.'

Her stomach churned. This was just awful, so much harder than she'd expected. Whenever she'd imagined finding Harry she'd pictured happy emotional embraces, apologies, heartfelt declarations of love. And kisses. Lots of kisses. She wanted to throw herself into his arms but he looked so remote and grim. 'When did you get back to Australia?'

'Yesterday.'

She nodded, clasped and unclasped her damp hands and ran them down her thighs.

Harry lifted his hips away from the railing and stood straighter, looking down at her. 'You have something in your hair,' he said, and a fleeting smile flashed in his eyes and then disappeared just as quickly.

Her hand flew to the top of her head. 'Is it yellow? It's probably paint. I've been painting the sun room.'

He cocked his head to one side, his gaze speculative. 'I didn't think you wanted to change anything about Alice's house.'

'Well... I got over that.' Jen gulped and looked out across the ocean to the huge green waves rolling towards the shore. 'I used to think that if I left everything the same that living in Alice's house would be as wonderful as it used to be when I visited her. But, of course, it's only a house. It takes people to...'

She let her vision follow the line of breakers and heard the loud thump as they crashed onto the sand, then the hiss as flurries of white foam raced up the beach. Why on earth were they talking about painting Alice's house?

Bringing her gaze back to him, she said. 'It's good to see you. I'm so glad you're here.'

A facial muscle worked close to his jawline. 'Why?'

'*Why?*' Jen repeated, amazed by his question. She opened her mouth to answer and then stopped, realising that her reply required care. With that one word Harry had asked everything.

They stood facing each other and Jen's heart pounded. She nodded and tried to swallow the huge knot of emotion that tightened her throat. Strain showed in Harry's eyes and in the downward tug of his mouth as he waited for her to go on. Her tongue slid over her dry lips. 'Now I can explain why I didn't reply to your letters.'

'You didn't read them,' he said, his voice flat, carefully devoid of emotion.

'No, I didn't.'

The skin around his mouth tightened and he shoved his hands in his pockets and looked away. 'That's what I figured.'

Jen touched his arm and he jerked his gaze back to meet hers. She was shocked by the steely hardness she saw there. 'I know this doesn't make sense, Harry, but I didn't read your letters until after they stopped coming.' She hoped against hope that he'd accept her explanation. 'I didn't read them at first because I was afraid. I thought they'd upset me, but I kept them and I've read them now. I've read them all, over and over.'

His eyes narrowed warily and she pressed a hand to her mouth to hold back a sob. 'I'm sorry,' she said, her voice breaking with emotion. 'I had no idea you felt like that. They're so incredibly beautiful.'

She heard the sharp rasp of his in-drawn breath. For an awful, horror-filled moment Harry stood staring at her as if he didn't believe her and she couldn't bear the tension any longer. She burst into tears.

With an agonised groan he drew her against him.

'Oh, Harry, I'm sorry,' she sobbed against his shoulder.

'Don't be, Jen. Don't be.'

'Am I too late?'

'Too late?' he repeated, brushing her ear with his warm lips.

'You said you loved me, but have you changed your mind?'

He drew back to look down at her, his eyes wide with surprise. 'About loving you?'

'Yes.'

'Oh, Jen,' he cried in a choked voice. 'How could you think that?'

He gathered her closer and she clung to him, drinking in the remembered smell of his skin and clothes, and feeling the wonderful strength of his muscles through the thin cotton of his shirt.

'I'm the one who should apologise,' he said. 'It was cowardly of me to run away to another country and then dish up my feelings in a bunch of letters. I should have been here. I should have been telling you face to face, showing you how much I love you.'

'I've missed you so much,' she told him. 'I've been so miserable without you. I almost lost my mind when I thought I'd lost you for ever.'

'Oh, brown girl.' Harry hugged her close, as if he were frightened she might disappear. She felt the wonderful, convincing strength of his need for her and an awful heavy weight seemed to shift from her heart.

The moment he released her she reached impulsive hands to either side of his head and drew his mouth towards hers. 'Kiss me, Harry.'

He brushed her lips with a butterfly-soft caress. 'If you'll say you'll marry me.'

'Stop teasing. Kiss me, or I'll die.'

He smiled and rubbed his nose against hers. 'Marry me, Jen.'

'Harry!' She captured his mouth with hers. Impatience, hunger, overflowing happiness. Love. Every pent-up emotion went into her kiss. And he kissed her back. No gentle butterfly sensations now. His lips were brazen, his tongue demanding, his mouth warmly, lovingly intimate.

When they broke the kiss at last he pressed his lips to her shoulder.

'Jen, Jen,' he whispered. 'You have no idea how much I want you.' She trembled as he scattered shiver-sweet nibbles along the line of her collar-bone till he reached the waiting hollow at the base of her throat. 'I love you.'

Then he pulled back and looked into her eyes. 'Put me out of my misery, Jen. Tell me one way or the other. This is all new for me. I've never proposed before. I'll do anything. I'm even willing to trade in my Harley for a lawnmower.' He touched the paint in her hair and grinned. 'Or perhaps a paintbrush.'

'Oh, goodness. Would you really do that?'

He frowned. 'You sound disappointed.'

'I was hoping you'd let me come travelling with you. I have this romantic notion that we could take off into the sunset and you could show me the world.'

Smile lines creased around his eyes and he began kissing her again. Oh, sweet heaven, would one lifetime be enough for his kisses?

'What about your job?' he asked much later. 'How will it fit with your plans to travel?'

'It can wait. I've been thinking of moving on anyhow—branching out on my own. I have clients lining up for my services—Lisa and Michael, for starters. They both want me to handle their publicity. And Jonno Rivers's brother, Gabe, is looking to expand his airline and wants help with promotion.'

'And I know a bloke called H R Taggart who couldn't manage without your special PR talents.'

She grinned. 'That's right. I'll be inundated with big name clients.'

Harry grinned back at her. 'OK. How's this for a plan? We get married and spend six months or maybe a year seeing the world and then afterwards you can take me home to your place and make me shepherd's pie.'

Jen's heart leapt halfway to heaven. 'It's a deal,' she said and, linking her arms around his neck, she lifted her face for yet another kiss.

*   *   *

The tall, dark, tuxedo-clad figure on the balcony adjoining the glittering ballroom watched the people inside while he spoke into a mobile phone. 'Hi, Caro, are you ready for some good news?'

'Harry—' came his mother-in-law's excited voice '—of course I am. What's happened?'

'Your clever, gorgeous younger daughter is Business Woman of the Year,' he said, unable to keep the pride and excitement from his voice. 'They've just finished the presentations.'

'Oh, how wonderful!'

'I can't get near my wife. She's the centre of attention at the moment—surrounded by journalists and politicians and celebrities.'

'So she should be. Look how many of their careers she's boosted,' said Caro. 'No one deserves this more. I'm so proud of her.'

'Ditto,' said Harry, grinning. He glanced at his wristwatch. 'So how's the babysitting going? Are the youngsters all in bed and asleep, or have you and Polly been spoiling them again?'

'They've been angels.'

Harry chuckled. 'I don't believe it. Millicent and Lisa's new baby might be angelic, but our two boys? Never.'

'Oh, Polly's got them sorted out. They'll do anything your grandmother asks them to.'

'That's true,' Harry admitted. 'She's never lost her touch for governing small boys.'

'Thanks so much for ringing, Harry. Now you go back and enjoy yourself.'

'OK. Thanks, Caro. We won't be home too late.'

As a dance band struck up a bright jazz number Harry pocketed the phone and strolled back into the ballroom, his eyes fixed on a slim laughing figure in a glamorous rust-gold gown. Jennifer Ryder, public relations consultant to the stars, Business Woman of the Year and mother of Jack and Xavier, the boisterous two-year-old twins.

His Jen. His brown girl. His remarkable, sexy, wondrous miracle. His wife.

He was gripped by a fierce impatience with the pack of outsiders gathered around her, but he forced himself to wait. This was her night, her moment. He needed to give her space, just as she'd given him his hour of glory on the night he'd won his literary prize in New York.

Lisa and Michael joined him, followed by Camille and Jonno, and they chatted and drank some more champagne in honour of Jen. An amazing number of people stopped by to pass on their congratulations and to slap him on the back.

His eyes searched the crowd for Jen again and suddenly, with the kind of telepathy that had become less surprising the longer they were married, she looked up and saw him at the precise moment he found her. Their eyes met across the crowded ballroom and her already smiling face glowed with sudden light. She waved.

He watched as she politely excused herself from the people closest to her and moved through the crowd, her eyes meeting his again and again, sending him smiles as she worked her way towards him.

Oh, God, he loved her. No one, except perhaps his grandmother Polly, could ever guess how important this woman was to him. He'd never, even with his rich imagination, thought that such depth of love was possible. Thank heavens he'd always run away from all the other women in his life. Somehow he must have known that there was just one perfect soul mate waiting for him.

As she drew closer their gaze held and he remembered the first time he'd seen her coming towards him through Maurice Mannix's crowded hairdressing salon. Everyone had been watching them that time, too. But this time he knew exactly what Jen wanted and what was going to happen next.

The message was in her eyes, in her softly parted lips, in her hands rising to link behind his neck. She wanted him. She wanted him to kiss her in front of all these folk and then she wanted him to take her home.

Harry smiled and opened his arms.

MILLS & BOON® PUBLISH EIGHT LARGE PRINT TITLES A MONTH. THESE ARE THE EIGHT TITLES FOR MAY 2004

❧

HIS BOARDROOM MISTRESS
Emma Darcy

THE BLACKMAIL MARRIAGE
Penny Jordan

THEIR SECRET BABY
Kate Walker

HIS CINDERELLA MISTRESS
Carole Mortimer

THE FRENCHMAN'S BRIDE
Rebecca Winters

HER ROYAL BABY
Marion Lennox

HER PLAYBOY CHALLENGE
Barbara Hannay

MISSION: MARRIAGE
Hannah Bernard

MILLS & BOON®

Live the emotion

0404 Rom LP

MILLS & BOON® PUBLISH EIGHT LARGE PRINT TITLES A MONTH. THESE ARE THE EIGHT TITLES FOR JUNE 2004

———— ❦ ————

SOLD TO THE SHEIKH
Miranda Lee

HIS INHERITED BRIDE
Jacqueline Baird

THE BEDROOM BARTER
Sara Craven

THE SICILIAN SURRENDER
Sandra Marton

PART-TIME FIANCÉ
Leigh Michaels

BRIDE OF CONVENIENCE
Susan Fox

HER BOSS'S BABY PLAN
Jessica Hart

ASSIGNMENT: MARRIAGE
Jodi Dawson

MILLS & BOON®

Live the emotion

0504 Rom L